SECOND CHANCE

"Society goes through many changes from time to time. Marriage is one such institution where it is facing new age challenges.
A second chance is needed to make it work, if the first one does not work out.
Looking through the eyes of Ragini the main character in the book, Dr Kavita Bhatnagar brings out a social issue all of us need to discuss, accept and support.
I wish Dr Kavita best wishes for the success of her book. Hoping to see it soon on best seller charts"

Dr. Radhakrishnan Pillai
Author - Corporate Chanakya

'Second Chance' puts contemporary challenges faced by today's woman in the Indian society to the fore. Ragini's fight with emotions, traditional values and her desires keeps you involved and makes you question the societal pressures.

Timsy Jaipuria,
Assistant Editor, CNBCTV18

'Second Chance' is a lucid tale of rapid transformation in the Indian social reality. Its lead character not only depicts emotional upheavals faced by a contemporary woman, but also a metamorphosis she has undergone because of her grit and sense of purpose.

Rajeev Jayaswal
Senior Editor, Hindustan Times

Second Chance.. It is a delightful book-easy to read yet conveys a strong message about a woman's right to make her choices....

Padma Shri Anju Bobby George,
Long jump World Championships Medallist

SECOND CHANCE

Kavita Bhatnagar

STERLING

STERLING PUBLISHERS (P) LTD.
Regd. Office: A1/256 Safdarjung Enclave,
New Delhi-110029. CIN: U22110DL1964PTC211907
Phone: +91 82877 98380
e-mail: mail@sterlingpublishers.in
www.sterlingpublishers.in

Second Chance
© 2020, Kavita Bhatnagar
ISBN 978 81 944007 5 2

This is a work of fiction. The names, characters and incidents portrayed in it are the work of the author's imagination and views expressed are personal of author. Any resemblance to actual persons, living or dead, events or localities, is entirely coincidental.

All rights are reserved.
No part of this publication may be reproduced, stored in a retrieval system or transmitted, in any form or by any means, mechanical, photocopying, recording or otherwise, without prior written permission of the publisher.

Editor: Sanjiv Sarin

Printed and Published in India by

Sterling Publishers Pvt. Ltd.,
Plot No. 13, Ecotech-III, Greater Noida-201306, U.P., India

To
My sister **Chitra**
For all the selfless love that she embodies

Contents

Prologue	7
The Perfect Man	11
DivorceeMatrimony.com	26
Life Is a Maze	38
I Am the Lord	50
Of Complaints and Bollywood	64
Kidney Beans	84
Two White Patches	97
You Only Live Once	107
Prince Charming	115
Second Chance	140
Second Chance 2	151
Happy Birthday	160
Epilogue	172

Prologue

Tears were rolling down her cheeks as Ragini entered the department store along with Kamini, her elder sister. The ride from the family court to the store had been completed in silence; both of them had been battling with multiple thoughts. The divorce was finally done legally, but whether it was really over and done with, only time would tell.

With that thought, she wiped her tears. Still distracted, she moved around, picking up stuff randomly and filling her shopping cart. The sound of soft sniffs behind her made her realize that Kamini, too, was crying.

With a sigh, Ragini reached out for a big packet of tissues.

At home later, curled up on the sofa with a hot cup of tea, she began to feel better, feel hopeful and alive. The cool air from the air conditioner further calmed her down. She decided to focus on the positive side of the situation. After all, she was only 26, pretty, intelligent, earning well and – divorced.

"In this age," whispered Kamini, more to herself than to Ragini, "being divorced is nothing unusual." She rubbed some hot oil in Ragini's long, thick, black hair and continued to speak gentle, caring words. Both Kamini and Ragini had inherited good looks from their beautiful mother. Tall and slim, with sharp features set well on a chiselled jaw line, both sisters had wheatish but clear complexions. The luscious hair, which they both wore long in plaits, was like their crowning glory. What set Ragini apart were her almond-shaped eyes that made her appear at once sensitive and intelligent and her warm, sunny smile that always made a lasting impact even on strangers.

As the wave of relaxation that accompanied the tender massage enveloped Ragini, she played her favourite CD of ghazals by Mehdi Hassan on her music system and listened with her eyes closed. As the soulful words of *"Ranjish hi sahi"* soaked deeper, Ragini regained her composure. She made tea again and sat quietly with Kamini. Each sip of tea made her feel more determined to remain positive, though her mind still alternated between the past and the present.

Marriage to Kadamb was in the past now. The marriage had turned out to be the absolute opposite of what she had dreamed it would be. She had been delighted to be selected as a probationary officer in the prestigious State Bank for Rural Development in Lucknow as she completed her MBA from Government College, Banaras. Her father and sister, who had still not come to terms with the sudden demise of her mother some years ago, felt happy as well. She would be starting work as a development assistant in a state-run bank, which was an achievement in itself. Her father moved in with Kamini, who lived in Banaras with her husband and four-year-old son, when Ragini shifted to Lucknow. She had barely begun settling in her job when Kadamb, a friend from college, proposed to her.

Nothing had prepared her for this turn of events in her life, but then, Ragini Mathur was a spirited girl and could not wallow in self-pity for long. After walking out and deciding to file for divorce, she had taken a small, rented apartment in Lucknow and settled in a routine where her job kept her busy. Luckily, her childhood friend Mia lived close by and they often spent their free time together. At nights, when loneliness took over, she thought about having a companion. In the year-long divorce process, she not only realized but came to a firm conclusion that she did not want to be alone. She was not deterred by the failure of her marriage to Kadamb. Something inside her kept telling her she deserved a second chance – for love, for togetherness, for happiness. Yes, she was very clear that she wanted to marry again.

It was with these thoughts that she reminded herself that now she was legally free to marry. As Kamini went off to sleep, with a wry smile Ragini reached for her latest acquisition – the Sony Vaio laptop and logged into the website second-marriage.com, a new portal focussing on second marriages, where she had registered herself some weeks ago and started updating her profile.

It's a jungle out there
Disorder and confusion everywhere
No one seems to care

Randy Newman

The Perfect Man

Ragini woke up with a start from her dream. It was 2 a.m. Kamini had left for Banaras a week ago and she was alone at home. She shuddered as she recalled her dream of being trapped in an aeroplane which was not able to take off and just kept taxiing on the runway. It was already becoming very hot, even though it was still April. She took a sip of water to calm herself down. To distract herself, she randomly picked up a book to read, and nodded in agreement as she read T.S. Eliot's famous quotation, "April is the cruellest month."

Indeed, the divorce was not going to be easy to live with. Although she had become used to staying alone, the recent decree of divorce made the memories of her marriage come alive every now-and-then. She recalled how she had tried to infuse a love of poetry in Kadamb and he had tried hard to enjoy reading poems with her. Her wandering mind made her forget the book in hand and took her to the past again.

She remembered how happy she had been when Kadamb had proposed to her.

Kadamb was a tall, reticent fellow with curly hair and decent looks. He was in her department, but a year senior. He had never overtly expressed his feelings to Ragini during college. So the proposal took her by surprise, but she had been fond of Kadamb a little, in her own way. During their group outings in college, she used to like the way Kadamb would hover around her as a protective figure. She had found him a sincere and caring friend and so when he proposed, she went ahead, thinking they were like-minded enough for the compatibility required for marriage even though their family backgrounds were different. Kadamb belonged to a well-known and well-to-do business family of Banaras, whereas Ragini's father was a professor. After an initial reluctance, seeing the willingness of both Kadamb and Ragini, their families had finally agreed to the marriage.

Ragini had been on cloud nine once the marriage was fixed and certain that she was going to get all the love she had dreamed of – her marriage would be perfect and she would really live happily ever after. However, her dreams soon turned sour as she realized the ugly truth behind Kadamb's sophisticated family. They were a money-minded, greedy lot who had expected monetary benefits from the marriage. The business was not doing well and they started taking Ragini's entire salary for use in their business. Even that was not enough and soon they started expecting Ragini to bring money from her father.

When these demands started, Ragini thought Kadamb would support her. She was astounded to see him being a mute spectator in the harsh treatment meted out to her when she refused to forward the monetary demands to her father. This was in complete contrast to the protective figure she had thought him to be. She questioned him but he simply shrugged off the responsibility saying that he could not go against his family. They were in financial trouble and they were only expecting help from her family. When her cruel mother-in-law started hitting her and yet Kadamb chose silence, Ragini walked out of the bitter, hurtful existence – shaken, but determined to create a new life for herself.

Her father had been aghast at her decision and was not in favour of a separation. He was even willing to give his meagre retirement savings to meet some of the demands of Kadamb's family but Ragini and other family members had not agreed to this. All this time, Kamini had been a pillar of support and strength to her. She had stood with her in her decision to end the abusive marriage when she saw that Kadamb was not willing to take a stand. She told Kadamb that they could slap a notice of cruelty on his family. Kadamb still did not respond. After an initial struggle for a solution, they agreed for a divorce with mutual consent and so after two years of marriage, in April 2005, Ragini was single again.

She recalled how Kadamb had shown no emotion when the court proceedings had concluded. In fact, his cold behaviour in the court had left her puzzled. Did he really have any feelings for her ever? Did he not have any anguish over the divorce, she wondered. Disturbed and unable to sleep or read any longer, she pulled her laptop to the bed and logged in. It was two weeks since she had posted her profile but there was no response so far. It could not be so bad, could it, she thought.

She decided to rephrase her rather sober profile and make it, as Mia would have said, " a bit more appealing".

Mia Gokhale was a vivacious girl, slender and attractive, with a mop of unruly brown hair which she wore short. Ragini smiled as she thought of the ever chirpy and also single Mia, who worked in a travel agency and was happy being with her numerous friends.

Suddenly she noticed that her inbox was showing some life – there was a message in the inbox! Hurriedly, she opened the message.

Hi there,
I saw your profile and liked it. You are welcome to go through mine and email me at atul 20 at yahoo dot com if you are interested.

Ragini noticed that he was not a paid member of the website and had smartly sent his email to her by camouflaging it as normal text. She then looked at the details.

Age – 32
Profession – Service (medical representative)
Place – Delhi
Marital status – Widower
Children – 1 daughter (4 years)

There was no photograph with the profile, leaving Ragini sufficient scope to dream of a tall, dark, handsome Prince Charming. But then the other details were enough to bring her back to reality.

She shut her Vaio and fell into deep thought. A widower with a daughter – is this what it will come to? Visions of being in a typical domestic situation where she was always tending to household chores and taking care of a child came to her. She had no experience of motherhood, so how could she suddenly become a mother to a four-year-old? She was almost going to reply "no, thanks" when she realized that this was the only message in her inbox. She had to take her chances. And so she answered.

Hi,
I have seen your profile. I think we can take it forward. However, I would like to have more details about your family and profession. I would also like to know about what you are looking for in a life partner. Will await your response.
Ragini
P.S. A photo would also be welcome :-)

She could not resist adding the last line, though the moment she sent the email, she wondered if it would make her look desperate. With those mixed thoughts, she returned to bed, grateful that it was a Friday and she did not have to get up early – there was no office on Saturday.

The new day brought some news. There was a notification for her on second-marriage.com.

Hi Ragini,
It is good to hear from you. I am Atul Sharma. I belong to a simple, middle class family of Gorakhpur

and my parents are still there. I work for M/s Kairo Products, a pharmaceutical company. As for life partner details, I am looking for a like-minded, simple lady, who obviously can be a mother to my daughter, Ria. My wife died in childbirth and since then I've taken care of her. Now increasingly, I feel the need to have a companion for myself as well as a mother for Ria. I liked your forthright attitude in the profile, apart from your good looks. The fact that your name started with the same alphabet as Ria, made me feel somehow that you will be a good mother to her.

I live in a rented house in Delhi and I hope we are able to connect and come together. If you want, you can call me on my mobile.

Regards

Atul

P.S. Incidentally, I am quite romantic by nature, though I may not sound so.

Ragini became immersed in thoughts. The guy appeared sincere and straightforward and sensible. Maybe ...

Ragini remained thoughtful as she went about her daily chores. She cleaned up her small apartment, went out to buy groceries and treated herself to a pizza at her usual joint – Pizza Choice. All the while, her mind was thinking of Atul. Maybe he is not good looking – that is why no photo. Will she be able to accept his daughter? Will the daughter accept her? What will her family say? Should she call Atul? Will she appear too forward if she calls? Will he think she is not interested if she doesn't call?

Ragini finally put a stop to all the questions racing in her mind. She decided not to appear too eager by calling Atul right away. She would call him after a decent delay.

At home, she busied herself in her favourite pastime – arranging her clothes in her cupboard. Somehow this activity of organizing always succeeded in calming her down.

The whole day passed in a whirl of emotions. She missed Mia, who was visiting her parents in Dehradun and was away for a few days. Kamini had returned to Banaras after being with her on the day of the divorce. Her husband Aman had asked her to stay with Ragini for a few more days, but her young son Shrey missed her. Besides, their father needed attention. She would call up Ragini daily, though. But when she called during the day and they chatted a bit, Ragini refrained from telling her about Atul.

The next day was Sunday. In the morning, the time appeared to pass ever so slowly. After delaying as much as she could, Ragini dialled Atul's number with trepidation, heart pounding loudly.

"Hello." Atul's voice was serious yet youthful and Ragini immediately liked it. They got talking and by the time they finished exchanging the basic notes about their lives so far, an hour had flown by. Atul was understanding about her divorce and Ragini felt sympathetic about his wife's passing away. She even heard his daughter in the background once or twice. At least he was truthful, she thought and put aside her anxiety about being a mother. She would cross that bridge when she came to it. Right now, it was more important to see whether she and Atul were able to relate to each other.

Atul extracted a promise from her to talk again after dinner. The day passed listlessly, with Ragini attempting to re-read *Not a Penny More, Not a Penny Less*, one of her favourite novels, dozing off now-and-then, and then returning to the novel. She found her restless mood turning towards elation as the evening drew to a close. Her loneliness was getting the better of her, she realized and tried to put a break on her thoughts.

Atul called promptly at 10 p.m. and before she knew, an hour had passed again. As she started to say goodnight, Atul whispered, "Come into my arms, dear, let me put you to sleep." Ragini was startled by the sudden intimacy and started to protest, but Atul reminded her that he had told her about his romantic nature. Ragini gave in after a while and experienced the powers of the virtual world as Atul spoke passionately to her and progressed to kissing her on phone.

Ragini had insisted that Atul send her a photo and her heart skipped a beat the next day when she saw an email from Atul. She also saw more responses for her profile, but in her happy state of being in love – well, almost – she didn't even open them.

Instead, she smiled smugly to herself when she saw Atul's photo. Was he handsome or was he handsome! He was perfect, the Raymond man personified, indeed. Ragini was thrilled and excitedly called up both Kamini and Mia to share her news. Kamini was surprised at the pace with which Ragini was rushing ahead, but at the same time she felt optimistic, too. She told her to exercise caution and not go overboard. Ragini, however, dismissed this as the usual elder sister's advice. Mia was excited and promised to come over as soon as she was back, to discuss in detail about Mr Raymond. Ragini then selected and emailed Atul some more of her photos, to which he responded with endearments.

Their intimacy on the phone grew in the coming days and Ragini became more and more certain that she had found love again. She was now smiling often, and more so when she caught herself in a mirror. Atul had made her very conscious of her "extreme good looks", as he called them. He had already professed his love for her thick hair, her warm smile and her slim yet curvaceous figure. His talks focussed a lot on lovemaking. Ragini often tried to shift the topic to more neutral subjects, but Atul would invariably manage to steer the conversation towards being virtually physical. He would ask what she was wearing, then proceed to undress her and explore every part of her, caress her tenderly, kiss her and then Ragini, growing uncomfortable, would disconnect the call. Coming from a conservative background, the explicit talks made her feel awkward. She felt Atul was going overboard, but not wanting to give up the opportunity to find a partner, she went along.

They had been interacting now for nearly two weeks and Atul appeared besotted with her. She wanted to really meet him and then move to the next stage of involving her family. Mia was still not back as her mother was ill. She talked to Kamini about it. Seeing her growing feelings, Kamini also advised her to meet Atul as soon as possible. In fact, Kamini had started teasing her about Atul and was also eager to meet him. And so, Ragini eagerly broached the topic with Atul over the now almost ritualistic, daily post-dinner call.

Atul was quiet for a moment and then said, "Ria's maid is on leave for a week. I will surely plan after that. I also so want to meet you, hold you and kiss you." His voice grew husky and passionate. Ragini also got entwined in his passion and the conversation took a different turn. It was only when she kept the phone down several minutes later that she realized that Atul had not agreed to come immediately, nor had he committed a date for his visit.

After a week, Ragini asked Atul again about when they could meet. He promised to inform her after a few days, after talking to his boss for leave. The next week, however, he told Ragini that he was not getting leave from office.

"I don't want to just come and go. I want to spend time properly with you ... stroke your hair ... lie down with you ... touch you all over ..."

Ragini cut him short this time and insisted that he come over to Lucknow during the weekend and meet her. Atul seemed to realize her firmness and agreed, although somewhat hesitantly, to book tickets and come by the Shatabdi Express the coming Saturday.

Ragini wondered what the reason could be for his reluctance. She remembered his ardent passion and blushed, telling herself that when he was so loving, she had no reason to doubt him. With that she shrugged off her doubts. There was nothing more she could do, anyway.

To distract herself, she started to prepare for the visit. She thought about where she should meet him. It would be better to meet at a restaurant first. But he would surely visit her home later. Ragini was also sure he would want to get physical with her, looking at the way he talked on phone. The question was, how far was she prepared to go? She was lost in her thoughts for a long time. Eventually, she decided to call up Mia, who was back and always gave her logical advice. Mia told her to relax and take things as they came. She added to her excitement by giving here encouraging tips to look her best and told her to think of what she would wear.

Ragini then went to the beauty parlour and got their latest facial done. She indulged in pedicure and manicure and in a hair spa. At home later, she tried out several outfits and kept the selected ones in her favourite pastels aside. She thought of where they would go and how the meeting would bring about clarity for the future. She had assumed that Atul would be there on Sunday as well and they would have many hours of togetherness. Perhaps, after a cosy dinner, they could catch a late-night movie too! She felt strange as she planned the time she would spend together with Atul and realized it was ages since she had gone out with a male friend. In all this time alone, her yearning for love and companionship had become stronger than she had realized and now she could barely control the excitement that was building up each day.

In her euphoric state, Ragini called up Kamini to share the news and told her about Atul's impending visit. She urged her not to tell their father yet. Kamini uttered words of caution but knew that the meeting was necessary before the next steps to finalize matters could be taken. And so Ragini spent the week enveloped in an air of anticipation, growing more restless as Saturday approached. Mia had to travel out again, this time for work and the lonely evenings made Ragini more edgy. Surprisingly, something seemed to be weighing on Atul's mind and he was not his usual lusty self in his phone calls.

Friday night arrived and as the customary after-dinner phone call came, Ragini was full of excitement – after this call, their next interaction would be face-to-face.

"Ragini, I won't be able to come tomorrow," was the first sentence she heard.

"Hellooo," she almost screamed. "What has happened now?"

"My uncle is very ill. He had a heart attack. I'm going to Mumbai tomorrow, I don't know when I will be back," Atul spoke in a very subdued tone.

"Ohhh ..." was all that Ragini could muster in response.

"Who will take care of Ria?" she asked after a moment, but the connection was already lost.

An ominous feeling came over Ragini as she sat down and tried to redial, but the call would not go through. Anticipation dissolved into tears and she sobbed her heart out – her dreams of meeting her Mr Perfect had come crashing down.

Still curled up on the sofa, she fell asleep in that state. She had fitful bouts of sleep, alternating between dreams of her chasing a taxiing aeroplane and Atul driving away in a car.

She woke up in the morning, troubled by her recurrent dreams. As she listlessly made tea, she wondered how she would pass the day. She tried to distract herself by searching, not for the first time, the meaning of her dream on the internet. The search results showed what they had shown previously – the dream of taxiing aeroplane signified being stuck in a situation with little escape. And stuck she felt.

Suddenly desperate for comfort, she grabbed the phone and called Atul. But his mobile was out of coverage area. Again, she felt a foreboding as if something bad was about to happen. Stubbornly, and with nothing else to do, she spent the entire day trying to call Atul, but in vain. The phone remained out of range. Ragini's frustration kept mounting.

Eager to know about the developments with Atul, Kamini called in the evening. On hearing the details and her distraught voice, she asked her to come down to Banaras immediately for a few days. But Ragini was in no state to think straight. She almost collapsed when, until late evening, her frantic calling yielded no results and Atul's number continued to be "not reachable".

She couldn't understand what had happened. Why did Atul come so close to her if he had no intention of even meeting her? Why all the talk, why the romance? A person who was virtually making love to her daily had simply vanished. She again turned to Kamini and shared her bewilderment and agony. Kamini, older and wiser, understood that her sister had been duped. Atul, if that was his real name, had only been having fun. She suggested to Ragini to call his office and ask about him.

Monday morning saw Ragini doing precisely that. She traced the office address and number and called, only to be told that no one called Atul Sharma worked there. She was aghast. She looked at his photograph and guessed it would be a fake one as well. She logged into second-marriage.com, but there was no trace of his profile now. And his mobile phone continued to be unavailable. He had simply disappeared in thin air, without a trace. Ragini remembered each and every conversation they had and felt foolish, vulnerable and hurt. She gave up attempting any further investigations.

Her head aching, Ragini tried to compose herself but it was too much for her to handle. She felt lonely and missed Mia and Kamini, both. She called Mia and shared all the details with her. Mia was full of rage and also cursed herself for being so naive. She should have asked Ragini to check at Atul's office in the beginning itself. Not wanting Ragini to be alone, she advised her to take a break and go to her sister. Kamini was also insisting this. So Ragini took leave from her office, packed her bags and went to Banaras. As she reached her sister's house, she crumbled again.

"Didi," she sobbed when Kamini opened the door, "I've been taken for a ride."

*****

DivorceeMatrimony.com

As dawn approached, Ragini walked down the narrow lane from her sister's house to her favourite Assi Ghat in Banaras. The small shops on the way were closed and the quietness calmed her. She sat on the steps by the edge of the water. She watched the changing colours of the sky, and admired how the waters in the river Ganges also changed hues. It was a sight she could never tire of watching but today her thoughts were reflective. The sight reminded her of the fact that in life too, one action impacts so many others.

As a child, when she had played around on these steps, she could not have imagined that divorce and the hunt for an ideal suitor were going to be such a large part of her destiny. She had always wanted a simple life but now she was at such crossroads where everything around was all but simple. As the waters continued to take on the colours of the clear, summer sky, her thoughts went back to her happy childhood.

Ragini remembered playing with Kamini, five years her elder, growing up in the winding lanes and the religious atmosphere of Banaras. Their mother was a typical homemaker, perpetually in the kitchen, with a penchant for keeping the home spic-and-span. Her father, a professor of English literature in the Banaras University, was a strict disciplinarian. He instilled a love for books in both the sisters, which they carried all their lives. They led a simple life, followed vegetarianism and typical middle-class ethos.

As Ragini came into her teens, she discovered her romantic nature, probably influenced by reading too many Mills and Boons, something which Kamini scorned. She would often fantasize about finding magical love and a perfect marriage. Around that time, she also developed a love for poetry. Kamini was the more rational of the two, and would dismiss Ragini's ideas about love, saying it was purely an illusion.

Ragini was very fond of seeing movies and would drag her mother and elder sister to the cinema whenever a new movie released. Fuelled by popcorn and coke and Bollywood melodrama, her dreamy nature became more profound and she soon developed a firm belief that her Prince Charming was waiting for her to discover. She developed a crush for the new superstar of the time – Anil Kapoor – and would see his movies several times. Ragini smiled as she remembered how angry her father had been on discovering her collection of Anil Kapoor's posters and photos and had thrown her precious collection away. She had sulked for days till Kamini promised to help in building the collection again. And so romantic notions of love had become an integral part of her from early years. At the same time, Ragini was better in studies than Kamini and academic success came easily to her. She was always the class topper and her father dreamed of a bright career for her.

Her mother's sudden demise after a brief illness had left them all shaken. As Kamini started taking more care of Ragini, their bond grew and both became each other's confidant. Gradually, Kamini had taken on her mother's role as Ragini finished her schooling.

A relative soon suggested a good match for Kamini and since the boy was based in Banaras itself, Kamini said yes, thinking it would enable her to take care of her father as well. Aman, a lawyer, was a caring and warm-hearted person. Ragini meanwhile had gone on to do MBA in finance. After she topped her MBA and was awarded a gold medal, Ragini's selection as a probationary officer in the State Bank for Rural Development at Lucknow surprised no one. Aman and Kamini decided then that her father would move in with them, as Ragini carved out a career for herself.

Ragini then remembered her joy at the time of marriage to Kadamb.

As a flood of memories engulfed her, she recalled how she had believed all her childhood dreams of finding love had come true. Kadamb had been a friend in college and had always come across as a decent, simple-minded person to Ragini. His family was affluent, being in the auto-parts business and all the friends knew that Kadamb would be joining the family business after MBA. Ragini and Kadamb would often go out with other friends for movies and outings but Kadamb had never asked her out for a date. She could sense that he liked her and she liked him as well, but in the absence of any direct hint from Kadamb, she was too shy to make the first move. Kadamb finished college and joined a firm in Lucknow to gain some experience before he joined the family business.

As her final year in college approached, Ragini became more occupied in preparing for competitive examinations. Upon selection, she joined the bank as a probationary officer with optimism. Their college had an active alumni group in Lucknow which she joined and met Kadamb again, along with a few other friends who were in the city. She could sense that Kadamb's feelings for her had grown and sure enough, Kadamb asked her out for a date and proposed to her. She wondered now if it was due to her bank job with a good salary, but at that time she had been full of happiness, thinking about a rosy life ahead.

Not wanting to dwell on her ugly marriage and bring back the painful memories, Ragini went across to the temple near the banks of the river but today even the gods could not give her any solace. She returned home in a forlorn state.

Kamini tried to fuss over her, but she remained moody. Her thoughts kept going back to Atul and how easily she had fallen prey to his false charms. She was also tormented by the realization that her emotional and physical needs had got the better of her and she had ignored her usually sensible self. Or maybe the divorce had made such a dent in her self-esteem that she was in a hurry to prove to herself that she was still desirable. Alone with these thoughts, she felt lost and without hope.

Kamini and young Shrey tried to distract her. Her brother-in-law, Aman, was also concerned and tried to cheer her up.

She steered clear of her father, who was too conservative to approve of any remarriage plans. Her father had not been in favour of her divorce but Kamini had played a major role in making him see Ragini's real condition in the hopeless marriage. He appeared to have withdrawn from Ragini and the bond between the father and the daughter had weakened a bit. It was Kamini, who had earlier filled the vacuum after their mother had passed away, who continued to provide solace to Ragini.

When it was time for Ragini to go back to Lucknow, Kamini turned emotional. "Promise me you will call every day," she said with concern. "Had it not been for Shrey's school, I would have come with you."

Ragini tried to smile, "It is okay, Didi. How long you will mother me? I will call regularly, don't worry." She said her good byes and prepared herself to face her loneliness.

The train journey back to Lucknow passed in a whirl of emotions. She reached home early in the morning and unpacked her bags. The trip had not really relaxed her. Her mind was still full of doubts. Should she continue her efforts to marry again? This question now dominated her thoughts as she joined back office and tried to focus on work. Didi had understood her needs and had told her to go ahead, but exercise a lot of caution. She had also promised to look for a suitable match for her among her friends.

A concerned Mia had rushed to meet her upon her return. Over dinner, as Ragini shared her ordeal, Mia told her to take things easy and not get so affected by her experience with Atul. The next evening, in a bid to make her feel better, Mia had dragged her to the beauty parlour.

Ragini's long tresses were constantly reminding her of Atul, who had often sung praises of them. She loved her hair and had always worn it long but now it was a painful reminder of Atul's lust and her foolishness. Ragini knew she had to do something about it. She looked at Mia and her short hair and she closed her eyes as she visualized what she was going to do. She had a word with the hairdresser and sat tense as the scissors began their action. Twenty minutes later, she looked in the mirror and smiled with satisfaction. Her hair was shoulder-length now, set in layers and she could flip it around with a toss of her head. She felt as if the action was making her worries disappear. The new look suited her more, Mia insisted.

Ragini felt rejuvenated. She felt she had broken her shackles and was liberated now. Gradually her moroseness disappeared and she applied herself enthusiastically to her new assignment in office, working hard for the research involved. She also deleted her profile on second-marriage.com.

The scorching heat soon gave way to the July showers and Ragini and Mia went out often, enjoying the famous street foods of Lucknow before the monsoon set in. Mia was dating someone she had met through a new dating site she had chanced upon. She did not find him interesting enough, while he was becoming obsessive about her. Mia would often strategies with Ragini about how to dump him and Ragini would marvel at her self-assurance.

Sensing Ragini's growing loneliness, Mia did some research and discovered Matrimony.com's match making service DivorceeMatrimony.com. Going by the reviews, it was a trusted website, one that verified accounts before posting profiles so that the chance of a fraud was minimized. She asked Ragini to register on this portal and reactivate her search.

So one evening, when Mia was around, Ragini picked up her laptop to look at this new site, but then she remembered the incidents of the past weeks and lost her enthusiasm. She shared her fears of being duped again with Mia, who understood them perfectly.

"Why don't you simply go on a date?" Mia suddenly asked. Ragini rolled her eyes, conveying her disinclination at Mia's proposal.

"With whom? I don't want to use any of your dating sites. I don't have the daring," Ragini replied.

"I know, darling and I am not suggesting that. I have someone I know in mind. Ram Kumar is an eligible bachelor in my office and he, too, is looking around. Though a bit of simpleton, you can just go out with him once and see for yourself."

Ragini mulled over the idea and finally said yes. There was no obvious harm in meeting a known guy from Mia's office. At least it would be safe. He wouldn't pester her for a second date if the first one didn't go well.

The response from Ram Kumar was an eager yes and Mia set up the date for Saturday evening at Pizza Choice, upon Ragini's insistence. At least the pizza would be good, if not the date, she said.

Ragini was not feeling very excited about her meeting but Mia, with her infectious energy, instilled some anticipation in her. She dressed in a trendy, pink salwar-suit and feeling smart in her freshly set hair, walked down to the restaurant a few minutes before the appointed time, to find Ram Kumar already there, waiting for her. Apparently, he had been waiting for some time. Mia had shown her his photograph, so she recognized him right away. He was average in looks but his simplicity had struck a chord in Ragini.

They greeted each other a little awkwardly and Ram seemed to be awestruck by her beauty. That felt good. Courteously, he asked her for her choices in pizza before ordering. Ragini settled for Veggie Delight.

As Ram looked lost for words, Ragini started the conversation. She tried to politely find out why he was still single and why he was showing interest in a divorcee. Ram wasn't much of a talker and was so smitten by Ragini that, in his nervousness, he could not muster a response, which made Ragini laugh. As they shared the piping hot pizza, their talk somehow veered around to demanding employers and poor-paying jobs. The travel agency Mia and Ram worked in was notorious for low salaries and Ram showed eagerness to know about Ragini's pay slip.

"You are earning a handsome amount, aren't you?" he asked, almost wistfully. "Your pay and perks are at par with the government officers. You are so lucky," Ram continued between bites of pizza. "We really slog in office all day but are paid peanuts. As of now, I can barely pay my rent, but together with your salary, life can be better," he concluded, with a satisfied smirk that Ragini could not make out was because the pizza was so good or because of the vision of her salary being spent by him.

She felt uncomfortable the way Ram presumed her interest and concurrence, but was too polite to say anything. Both Mia and she had taken him to be a simpleton, but here he was, talking about salaries on the very first date. The conversation was already reminding her of how her former in-laws had behaved with her over money. With not much else to talk about, the evening ended quickly, to Ragini's great relief.

Ragini walked over to Mia's home. Mia was lounging on her sofa, watching TV. She threw a pillow at the perplexed Mia and narrated the whole episode to her. Mia burst out laughing.

After a moment, Ragini saw the humour and joined in, the laughter taking away her annoyance. Ram was a joker, they concluded. Together, they shredded the money-minded Ram Kumar to pieces. Ragini felt lighter and Mia wanted to make her resolve to enjoy her singlehood for the time being. Ragini, however, showed keenness to register her profile in the new website that Mia had found and so both friends created a brief profile on DivorceeMatrimony.com.

Mia was both bemused and perplexed at Ragini's almost obsessive need to remarry. She and Ragini had gone to the same school in Banaras and though temperamentally different, had always shared a strong bond. Mia was fiery and independent and felt protective towards Ragini, who was more emotional and dreamier. Mia and her parents had shifted to Dehradun by the time the girls entered college, but they stayed in touch and were delighted to discover that they would both be working in Lucknow. They had even thought of sharing a flat together, but that did not happen since Ragini had got married.

Mia remembered how she had teased Ragini about leaving her in a lurch in her keenness to marry Kadamb. Ragini had not really evaluated Kadamb's proposal properly and had been so enamoured by the thought that love was coming her way that even when Mia tried to tell her to give it more time and enjoy a courtship period, Ragini had not paid heed to it. Mia recalled the huge, traditional wedding in Banaras. Ragini's father had left no stone unturned for the grand arrangements. Ragini had looked beautiful and radiant in her bridal attire and her eyes had never left Kadamb the entire evening. No one had foreseen the events that would follow.

Ragini had been brave and courageous throughout the divorce process. Since they had cited incompatibility and irreconcilable differences as the reason, they had to go through the customary counselling. Ragini had feigned indifference to the process but at times shared her turmoil with Mia. Kadamb had been completely emotionless throughout. Mia had wondered where the love had flown. Probably it wasn't there in the first place, she decided.

Kamini would often come down to Lucknow to accompany Ragini and Mia for the hearings and would break down at times, worrying about Ragini's future. Mia had marvelled then at the strength in Ragini that made her so stoic throughout. Never once did she waver in her resolve, and if she worried about her future, she did not let it show often. Rather, she tried to make light of it all as much as possible. It was in one such moment, towards the end of the divorce process that she had registered herself on the matrimony website which specialized in second marriages, making her determination to remarry very clear. While Kamini had accepted this as inevitable, Mia recalled how both sisters had anticipated their father's reluctance for a second marriage and had decided not to share all the details with him. And now that Ragini was seriously looking at suitors, Mia wondered how it would turn out. The world was not as simple as her friend was. After Atul's deception, she had wanted Ragini to relax and just enjoy meeting people, but she had not succeeded. Ram's behaviour had made her task more difficult. Why couldn't two people simply meet as friends?

Mia sighed as she thought all this and hoped fervently that her friend would find what she was looking for soon, without hurting herself more.

*****

Life Is a Maze

After a tiring day in office, Ragini tried to go sleep early, but couldn't. After some hours of no sleep and tossing and turning for some time, she got up from the bed. Her resolve to stay single weakened. She remembered her new profile on DivorceeMatrimony.com and she told herself she would only log in and surf – nothing beyond it.

Her inbox showed two messages received soon after her registration. She rejected one of them outright as it had too many grammatical errors – English had to be good, after all. The other showed some promise.

Name	:	Raj Kumar
Age	:	34
Marital Status	:	Single
Profession	:	CEO, RKS Infodreams
Place	:	Ahmedabad

The bare profile read almost like a visiting card, thought Ragini. His message was also very basic, asking for her details and areas of interest.

> I am a simple guy with simple interests. I belong to Banswara, Rajasthan but am now settled in Ahmedabad. I did my engineering from LD College of Engineering, Ahmedabad and then started my own company in software exports – you can see more details on the website rksinfodreams.in.
> More when you revert.

Since Ragini had not responded, he had sent a reminder, which was almost ten days old.

Ragini first checked the webpage he had mentioned. To her relief, the details of the company and its CEO were all there and looked genuine. Still, Ragini made a mental note to reconfirm the information by calling the listed telephone numbers in the morning. There was a photograph of Raj on the website which showed him to be almost a middle-aged person – or older, if the photograph was not a recent one. He had a dark complexion and slick, black hair. Ragini didn't particularly like his swarthy looks, but then reminded herself where the previous good-lookers had landed her. Honesty and sincerity were more important, she told herself.

Hesitatingly, Ragini typed out a reply.

I'm looking for a gentle and caring life partner who is well settled in life. I have had a bitter first marriage and I do not want to repeat any such bitterness in my second choice. I would like to know more details like when you passed out from engineering college, where you studied before that, who all are there in your family and what are you looking for in your life partner. Also, since you have posted a profile on DivorceeMatrimony.com, what about your first marriage?

Looking forward to your reply.

Ragini

She wondered if her forthright message would get a reply. The proposal was anyway two weeks old now.

But the reply came the next day itself.

> Hi there,
> Good to hear from you! I was wondering at the silence and had almost given up hope.
> Phew, a barrage of questions from you. Let's talk and discover each other more. I'll be happy to call you if you share your number.
> Regards,
> Raj

Ragini was very clear she didn't want to give her mobile number. She remembered her intimate conversations with Atul. "Never again!" she told herself firmly and sat down to reply.

> I think emails are an equally a good way to discover each other initially. If you have a problem with this, we can wait and meet when possible and then take this further.

The rather curt reply somehow made her happy. She felt in control and found herself even humming a song. She called up the office number of RKS Infodreams and posing as a client confirmed that Raj was indeed the CEO of the company.

There was no reply for a couple of days. Meanwhile, Mia came over and gave her some more insights about the world of dating.

"Ragini, you are such a simple soul," said Mia. "Why are you stuck to this marry again business? You are young and single. Meet people, go out, just have fun."

Mia valued her single status a lot and didn't intend to marry – not in the near future, anyway. She often got irritated with Ragini's urge to marry again and thought she should simply enjoy life. She continued to push Ragini.

"You sign up at a dating site like simply-friends.com," said Mia in her enthusiasm, forgetting that it was she who had introduced Ragini to DivorceeMatrimony.com. "You will meet people of your age, in your city. Just start going out and you never know what it might lead to."

Ragini brushed aside the idea of casual dating. She didn't want to complicate her life. Her simple goal was to get married again. In fact, her youthful fantasy of an ideal marriage had never really left her and she could never fathom the reason for it. Love and marriage were her two prime needs in life and even a divorce had not been able to change that. She did not believe in the "single and ready to mingle" way of life. Stability and commitment were important to her. And so she was willing to wait and continue searching till she found her true love. She could not do what Mia suggested.

Raj replied after a few days saying that he understood Ragini didn't want to talk on phone. He said he might be travelling to Lucknow after some time and if it was okay, he would like to meet her then.

Ragini liked the sensitivity he had displayed towards her preference. She continued with her fact-finding mission. She called up LD College of Engineering to verify if Raj was their alumni. Thankfully, she got a positive reply. He had indeed graduated from there. Ragini was relieved. Only then did she agree to meet him.

A few days later, Raj emailed that he was visiting Lucknow after a couple of days. Ragini grew excited. She called up Kamini and told her about it. Kamini suggested her to meet him along with Mia, but Ragini didn't want to do that. Mia advised her to meet him with an open mind and assess his suitability to her needs. And so a couple of days later, after office, she found herself at Honeydew, a popular restaurant in Hazrat Ganj, trying to locate Raj.

She spotted him at a corner table and he also recognized her from her profile picture. While he merrily waved out to her, she again found his looks a put-off. She didn't particularly like his huge nose and dark lips, which looked like the result of too much smoking. She visualized going out together with him and was convinced it was a mismatch.

He didn't seem to notice her reaction at first and started chatting animatedly, with Ragini replying half-heartedly in monosyllables. Soon, sensing her unease, Raj said, "There's no compulsion, Ragini. You don't have to reciprocate, just because I like you. You can say no and leave if you want."

Embarrassed, Ragini pulled herself together and told herself that looks were not everything. Raj appeared sincere, sensitive and genuinely interested in her. He was also doing well in life. What more did she want?

She mumbled an awkward apology to Raj and demurely asked where they would meet the next day. Raj's eyes lit up and he reached out for her hand to convey his feelings. They decided to eat a light meal and only have a soup and a salad. Raj talked of his struggles in setting up his company and said it had left him no time to find a partner. It was because of his age – he was almost 35 – that he thought he would find a more suitable match on a second marriage website. Ragini pondered about their age gap while she tried to keep the conversation going. She spoke about her job and her family and obviously avoided any mention of Atul. Soon the dinner was over, and they agreed to meet at the famous Bhul Bhulaiya the next day.

That night Ragini fell into a relaxed sleep, after many troubled nights. This itself was a reassuring sign, she told her sister as she narrated the meeting the next morning. Kamini pointed out the eight-year age gap between them, but then said some compromises would anyway have to be made. In spite of everything, Ragini felt optimistic.

After office the next day, she hurriedly rushed home, changed from her office suit into jeans and shirt and took an auto to the Bhul Bhulaiya. Raj was already there and this somehow pleased her. He took her hand again as they entered the maze. After a while he commented, "Life is such a maze – you never know what turn it will take next." Ragini smiled at the trite metaphor. The next thing she knew was Raj on his knees, asking her if she would marry him.

She was dumbfounded, totally unprepared for this. But the romantic in her took over and she gave in to the moment. She found herself saying yes, though her mind said she should ask for some time. As Raj took her in his arms, she sighed contentedly.

While returning home in Raj's cab, he told her he was leaving the next day and Ragini agreed to see him off to the airport. He then looked at her solemnly and said, "Listen, one more thing. Every month I will be sending a fixed amount of money to Banswara. You will never question me on that."

Surprised, Ragini asked, "Why? I mean why will you send the money and why will I not ask? And where is Banswara, anyway?"

Raj didn't answer immediately. Then after a few minutes he said, "I'm asking you not to question this. I'm going to take care of you and this sending money to Banswara should not impact our relationship. You will have to trust me. That's all."

Ragini felt strange, but didn't say anything. She got down as her home approached and waved a goodbye to Raj.

She felt uneasy at the curious requirement Raj had put up and wondered what the real reason could be. As sleep eluded her, her mind remained active. Should she accept the condition? Will Raj turn away if she didn't accede to his request? Was her need for marriage so much that she was considering brushing aside something that sounded so wrong? What if there was something sinister behind it? Confused and unable to decide, she called up Mia.

As soon as she dialled Mia's number, she realized it was 2 a.m. Mia picked up the phone on the first ring. Maybe she too couldn't sleep. After hearing what Ragini had to say, Mia was very suspicious about the whole thing. She told Ragini to reconsider her hasty decision of accepting the marriage proposal and find out more about Raj. Ragini agreed with her. Exhausted, she finally fell asleep.

Early morning, the sound of the doorbell ringing loudly woke her. She rushed out to find Raj there, his earlier poise missing. "I've decided," he announced as he came in, "let's get married right now."

"Right now?" Ragini was astounded. She thought he was joking but then she saw the garlands he was carrying in a bag and she was suddenly frightened. Was he actually crazy?

"Yes, right now," Raj continued forcefully. "What's there to wait for? We like each other. You said yes yesterday. Let's do it now. Let's go to the nearby temple. I have got the garlands – you get ready quickly."

He brushed aside Ragini's protests about her family and told her they would both go and seek their blessings once it was done.

Ragini went to her room, wondering how to deal with this catastrophe. How could she do this? She was not prepared for it at all. Raj was really daft to think marriage could be done like this. And what about that strange condition about sending money?

She quickly texted Mia to come over and save her from this madman. Mia came over within minutes and asked what was going on.

"He wants us to marry now itself," Ragini said.

"Very good," responded Mia. "We will need two witnesses. Should I call my uncle – the DIG of Police and ask him to be a witness? He will also help to smoothen the process."

Raj's face went white at the mention of police and he looked at Ragini. Gathering courage, she told him that she couldn't marry like this. Her family had to be involved and present for the ceremony.

"Well then," Raj said, "looks like we are not meant to be together. You don't trust me." He left the house hastily and Ragini sank down on the sofa, totally shaken.

Later, Mia analysed the situation. "Look, you met him on DivorceeMatrimony.com. He must have a wife hidden somewhere, to whom he sends money every month. And seeing a pretty damsel like you, he didn't want to take a chance. He wanted to force you into marriage before you had second thoughts," she said.

Ragini felt Mia was right. Even if she was not, while she wanted to marry, but certainly it could not be like this.

Mia tried to show Ragini the funny side of her attempt to marry again. To take her mind off, she made Ragini wear a pretty yellow-coloured suit and took her shopping, "Nothing like retail therapy," she said. They went to a popular mall and shopped around for clothes, the activity relaxing Ragini. Sipping iced tea later, Mia shared her own experience of the dating site she was using.

"This guy was really cute, so I just agreed to go

to a movie with him. We cuddled and got real cosy during the movie. Then, as he was persuading me to go for a drive with him, his mobile rang. And I could make out that his wallpaper had the photo of a pretty woman with a child. When I asked him who they were, he said they were his sister and her child. Tell me, how many men you know would put a photo of their sister and nephew as their wallpaper? Obviously, the guy was married and was lying to get me into bed. So my dear, relax, at least this guy wanted to marry you." Hearing that, Ragini felt a little relieved at her escape and dismissed marriage attempt episode number two from her mind. Feeling better, both friends went to their homes.

Though Mia had made light of the incident, she was worried by the way Ragini was being lured by persons trying to exploit her desire to marry again. Were there no normal persons around? Why only imposters and weirdos? As Mia settled down to sleep, her thoughts went back to events that happened some years earlier.

While Ragini was struggling with her first marriage, Mia was living a different life. Living alone made her feel liberated – something she had always aspired for. She wanted to enjoy her freedom to the maximum. Ragini had become withdrawn due to the problems she was facing in her marriage. Their meetings had also reduced. Mia was left alone in the evenings. She joined a gym and focused on improving her already slender figure.

Within a few days, she found herself drawn to

the young and muscular gym instructor and started vying for his attention. Samir noticed her too and soon they went out on a date. Mia still remembered every detail of that evening. She remembered how Samir had taken her to a restaurant where they had enjoyed a delicious Italian meal. Then they went for a drive and he took her to his home, a small bachelor's pad. It had all been very exciting to Mia. They had kissed wildly and Samir had wanted to go on. Mia had barely managed to stop him, reminding him that it was only their first date.

After that they started to meet regularly and soon Mia was madly in love with him, wanting to marry him and making no bones about it. Sam, as she had started calling him, had no such intention and only wanted to have some fun. He cleverly led Mia on and they became lovers, Mia surrendering to him completely and hoping that this would make him propose to her.

She had wanted to share it all with Ragini but Ragini had her own problems. She had been so disturbed all the time that she had taken leave from office and had gone to Banaras so that the space between them could make Kadamb see some sense. Mia hoped with each passing day that Samir would propose to her and followed him around like a devoted puppy. But Samir soon started distancing himself and made it clear that he was not interested in marriage. Bitter arguments followed and Samir was brutal in dismissing Mia from his life. A heartbroken Mia cried for days in solitude.

Finally, she took charge of herself. She would become immune from all this marriage business, she decided. If Samir could have fun, so could she. She exerted all her will power to end her despondency. One of the first things that she did was to ask a colleague to pretend to be her boyfriend. She went arm-in-arm with him to the gym and made sure that Samir saw them. Point made, Mia pledged never to be in that situation again and never get exploited for the sake of love and marriage.

Much later, she had shared the incident with Ragini and told her that she had learnt her lessons. She could not fathom why Ragini was not able to learn that lesson as well and focus on her own self. For her, one incident had been enough to transform her. But Ragini, after an abusive marriage, was going through one troublesome episode after another in her bid to remarry. She decided to have a firm talk with her soon and wean her off from this madness.

*****

I Am the Lord

Ragini narrated the entire episode about Raj to her sister. Kamini was scared of where it might have led to. "You must stop these experiments," she said. "Papa is not even aware that you are up to all this. He will be very upset with me if he found out that I knew all this all along and didn't tell him or stopped you."

Ragini begged her to continue to support her and promised she would be more cautious in the future. Kamini agreed, though reluctantly. Ever since Ragini's divorce, she had become the bridge between her sister and her father, balancing their relationship and ensuring that no conflict took place. Even otherwise, she had always been supportive of Ragini and worried a lot about her.

After the divorce, Kamini had wanted Ragini to take a transfer to Banaras but Ragini had refused. "Didi, you cannot take all responsibility for everyone, always," she had insisted and Kamini had given in. She understood Ragini's needs and wanted her to be happy. She was even working on her father to make him accept that Ragini may marry again.

Ragini busied herself in office work, not visiting her profile at all. She tried to prepare herself to live her life alone. Mia had a long and serious conversation with her.

"Look, I know you want to remarry but don't be in this tearing hurry," Mia said over a cup of tea. "Your Prince Charming will turn up one day, but till then don't hurt yourself, trying to think that every man you meet could be the one."

Ragini was touched by her concern but her desire to find a companion was so strong that Mia's advice fell on deaf ears.

"I know the Samir incident turned you off marriage and by the same logic my failed marriage should have been enough to keep me away from trying again," Ragini said in a serious tone. "But there are two issues that make me 'stubborn', as you say," she went on. "The first is that divorce has made me feel rejected and inferior. I feel that only by finding love will my self-esteem be restored. It's like what you did by taking a false boyfriend to Samir. But I want my partner to be genuine. And second, you will agree that we all need a companion. I feel marriage gives stability and that's why I don't want to adopt your approach. And mind you, the danger to hurt yourself is very much there in your approach too," Ragini concluded, sounding much wiser than she felt.

Both friends fell silent, each thinking about the way of life they had chosen. Mia had always been protective towards Ragini. She realized that Ragini needed her support now more than ever. She decided to ensure that Ragini didn't go into depression over her failed efforts and also make sure that nobody took advantage of her. So she often came to rescue her from bouts of loneliness and once even accompanied her to an astrologer.

Ragini had seen a large advertisement in the newspaper about the miraculous powers of Kashi Baba, who could solve any of life's problems. While she did not believe in astrology or any such mumbo-jumbo, the advertisement kept haunting her. Impulsively, she booked an appointment for herself and then dragged Mia with her to visit the Baba.

They were greeted by chants extolling the virtues of Baba as they entered Baba's den. Ragini felt optimistic, but Mia was sceptical. Kashi Baba was a typical baba – bearded, garlanded and bare chested – for he unravelled his bhaktas' future for them. And as Ragini discovered, all the while charging hefty amounts from them for making life easy and better.

Respectfully, Ragini went forward and touched his feet, asking him whether a second marriage was in her destiny. Baba rolled his big eyes before closing them and went into a trance. Some moments later he opened them and pronounced, "You will definitely remarry, but when it will happen is not certain as your stars are hazy. You will have to do some rituals to cleanse your stars, only then the details of remarriage will emerge."

He then asked for ₹20,000 for performing the prayers, which would clean Ragini's stars enough for her to get married quickly. Before Ragini could say anything, Mia interrupted, sought some time from Baba to decide and almost pulled Ragini out of the room.

"Be sensible," she told Ragini.

Ragini realized she was being silly and put away all thoughts of Baba from her mind. She was, nonetheless, consoled by Baba's prediction that a remarriage would happen in future.

Feeling motivated, she again logged into her profile and saw there were three messages in her inbox. She discarded one as he was not even a graduate. The second one was a businessman in Indore but his balding, ageing looks put Ragini off. The third profile appeared interesting.

Prabhat Soori was an investment banker based in Denver, Colorado. A divorcee with two children, he was 35 years old. His profile said nothing else but showed his plush home and his children. Though Ragini found him appealing, she was aware of the complications that engaging with him could entail. Dealing with two children in a foreign land was definitely something not easy. However, his message caught her attention.

> Dear Ragini,
>
> I came across your profile and liked what you have stated. I have been through a divorce too and understand the pain that accompanies it. My children live with their mother in Denver itself and I exercise my visiting rights. I am looking to remarry for the prime sake of having a companion for myself. I earn decently well and can take care of you in all aspects. Please feel free to email or call me at the given details, in case you want to take this further.
>
> Regards,
>
> Prabhat

Ragini noticed that he was a premium member of the website which enabled him to send his contact details directly. She also liked the way he had explained his situation. The age gap was a deterrent, though. Ragini decided to reply to him in a cautious manner and first get details of his profession, divorce and lifestyle from him.

Dear Prabhat,

Thank you for your message. Your profile appears interesting but I have a lot of questions from my side. Why did your divorce happen? Being in the same city and being the mother of your children, you must definitely be interacting with your ex-wife. That may be an issue with me. Moreover, your lifestyle must be very different from mine. I have a job here, which I may not want to leave and also, I have not yet thought about leaving India and going far away from my family. I am a vegetarian and a teetotaller and this must be acceptable to you. You would also have expectations from your future spouse, which I would like to know. We can interact further if you like and try to find a common meeting ground on these matters.

Regards,

Ragini

Ragini sent the email but her mind was churning. If Prabhat was as sincere as he sounded, was she willing to adapt so much and change her whole life? She wasn't sure.

She went to her office and immersed herself in her work, keeping all other thoughts at bay. In the evening, she first called up Kamini and shared the details of Prabhat with her. "Didi, I'm feeling uncertain about it," she concluded.

"It is but natural to feel so. Marrying an NRI has its own issues. There are two children involved. So weigh all aspects carefully and don't rush up things," Kamini advised, indirectly alluding to the past episodes. Mia also told her more-or-less the same thing and asked her to exchange views rationally with Prabhat. She also suggested background checks and Ragini wondered how she was going to do that.

Sighing, Ragini checked her account and saw that there was no response from Prabhat. "Maybe he also realized that how difficult it was going to be to go ahead," Ragini thought and drifted off to sleep.

In the morning, when she checked again, she found a reply from Prabhat in her inbox.

Dear Ragini,

I understand your questions but I don't have answers to many of them. My divorce happened mainly due to cultural differences as I remain largely a traditional Indian. I wanted to raise the kids in that manner, which was not acceptable to my ex-wife. So we parted ways. But I could not get custody of my children and I feel I lost out on whatever little I could have otherwise contributed to their lives. I have to let bygones be bygones and I am ready to move on now. Yes, if we progress further, you will have to relocate to Denver, leaving your job and family behind. Also, to be honest, I'm not really sure if I want more children. I would rather focus on getting the custody of my kids back and be with them in the way I want to be. Think about it and let me know your response.

Regards,

Prabhat

Ragini read his reply and let two days pass before she firmed up her mind. On one hand, she liked Prabhat's forthright approach. He was also well-qualified and doing well. On the other hand, she knew she wanted children of her own. She also did not want to deal with all the baggage that Prabhat was clearly hinting at. Her career was important to her. So after carefully weighing all aspects, she sent a brief email to Prabhat stating that it could not work out and wishing him luck.

Kamini and Mia appreciated her stance and told her to be patient. Ragini felt relieved that there had been no emotional damage in dealing with Prabhat and tried to take each day as it came.

However, as days passed, Ragini started feeling restless. Her fears of being alone returned and she felt perturbed. What was she to do? Was she destined to live her life alone? Were all colours of romance and love to vanish from her life? It wasn't fair. She had come to know through a friend that Kadamb was getting married soon and this had further deepened her pain. It reinforced her belief that Kadamb had never truly loved her and that is why he had let her go so easily. The divorce was not her fault, yet she was the one suffering from loneliness. She wondered what the solution was.

"The solution," excitedly informed Kamini one day, "has been found!"

She had called Ragini late in the night. It transpired that Aman's sister, who knew about Ragini's situation, had recommended her husband's distant cousin, based in Kanpur, as a probable suitor. Since it was a known family, it would be a big plus in convincing their father, said Kamini. Ragini felt happy. She again saw a ray of hope. Maybe this method was better and an arranged marriage would be more suitable, looking at what she had been experiencing in the world of internet.

Kamini gave her more details. Deepak Shrivastav was 33. He belonged to a small family – only his mother and younger sister stayed with him. His father had passed away a few years ago. He was running their family business of textile printing in Kanpur.

"But why he is still single?" Ragini wondered out aloud. Suspicion had started coming easily to her now.

"It seems he is a bit fussy," replied Kamini. "He wants a near-perfect bride – a mix of homely and modern, job and home management both, good looking, able to take care of his mother, able to follow their family value system and so on."

"Well," said Ragini," apart from the age factor, this MCP attitude itself is enough to refuse him." But Kamini candidly told her to look at her options – which at the moment were precisely zero. Marriage itself was a compromise, and here they were dealing with a second marriage. In fact, Ragini should take it as a compliment if he agreed to marry her, Kamini concluded forcefully.

Ragini almost fought with her on this statement. But Kamini managed to pacify her saying that there was a good chance that their father would agree for this match. He might say no to others. Ragini relented, finally, seeing Kamini's enthusiasm and agreed to meet Deepak. The meeting would be in Banaras, so Ragini took leave from office and went to Banaras a day earlier.

Kamini's house was looking spruced up when Ragini arrived. Kamini took her to their father, who was waiting for her. Principally, he was not in favour of a second marriage. His thinking was a little conventional. Hence, so far he had stayed away from talks of remarriage. However, as Kamini had guessed, since the proposal had come from her in-laws, it could not be dismissed without a serious consideration.

"A lot of adjustments are needed in any marriage," said her father, "and in your case it should be a situation of once bitten twice shy. Say yes only if you are convinced you will be able to adjust and compromise. To marry again is a very serious affair. I've already had to explain a lot to relatives and neighbours."

Ragini felt the unfairness of the comments but kept quiet. She was already developing an aversion to this Deepak. Hopefully he would not find her good enough so that she could avoid the awkwardness of saying no.

The Shrivastavs were to arrive by lunch time the next day and then stay the night. When Ragini woke up early in the morning, Kamini was already busy in the kitchen. The aroma of potatoes being fried filled the house. Ragini also started helping her.

"Wear that pink sari which we bought from Apsara. Pink really suits you," said Kamini.

"What else, Didi? Should I enter the drawing room with my head covered and a tea-tray in my hands?"

"Not a bad idea," Kamini said in mock seriousness and Ragini glared at her.

The Shrivastavs arrived punctually at 1 p.m. Ragini peeped out from behind the door of her bedroom as her family welcomed them. Deepak was average in looks, she decided, with a wheatish complexion, nondescript features and a stout build. He appeared confident, even a little overbearing. The mother and the sister walked behind him and looked decent and simple. The sister was, in fact, rather sweet in looks but had an air of helplessness around her.

Her father started to speak first, detailing with pride their family lineage. Her brother-in-law asked Deepak about his business. Then sensing that Deepak was getting restless, Kamini called in Ragini. After greeting everyone, Ragini sat next to her sister, aware of Deepak's piercing gaze, as if scrutinizing every bit of her. As she had never gone through this "arranged marriage" experience before, she had told herself that she would sit back and enjoy it. After all, it was not a college exam.

"So Ms Ragini," began Deepak, his voice as pompous as his bearing, "I realize you have been through an unfortunate experience. It is bound to have impacted you. Are you ready to take care of new responsibilities now?"

Ragini was irritated by his, "I'm the Lord" attitude but hid her feelings and asked politely, "What kind of responsibilities?"

She listened to Deepak elaborate upon the duties of a good wife and homemaker. He pronounced himself as a progressive man who did not want to quiz her on her past as the future was more important. His mother and the sister kept quiet all this time and Ragini almost felt sympathy for them.

Lunch was announced. Deepak continued his monologue at the table, switching to his likes and dislikes in food. "I like only home-cooked food," he declared as he took big helpings of the sumptuous-looking dum aloo, matar paneer and dahi-vada.

"And one more thing is very important in my home," he said, "the dough should be kneaded fresh everyday by the lady of the house. This is important not only from the health point-of-view but also from the astrological angle as it increases the prosperity of house."

"What absurd ideas," thought Ragini. She had visions of herself kneading dough and making food day-and-night, with no respite. And if his appetite was anything to go by, she would never stop cooking. Politely, she asked him of his view on having help at home in the form of a maid.

"Maids can only be of limited help, so why waste money on them?" he responded. " After all, a maid won't get up at five in the morning to fetch fresh milk from the dairy. It is the women of the house who have to attend to such tasks without fail."

Ragini looked at Kamini, who was also shocked and did not know where to look. It was amazing that such a closed mind existed in today's world.

In the evening Deepak asked permission from Ragini's father to take her out for a cup of tea. Though Ragini had made up her mind to say no to the proposal, curiosity made her go on this "date". She soon found out the reason behind this outing. Deepak started speaking about sex, not looking her in the eye but focussing on the cup of steaming tea before them.

"Physical intimacy is something sacred," he said. "I am very religious by nature and on Mondays, Tuesdays, Wednesdays and Saturdays, I do elaborate prayers. As my wife, you have to assist in them. These prayers are done to balance my astrological chart and the position of stars to increase my health and prosperity."

"That is very good," interjected Ragini.

Deepak became quiet. His face went red and he seemed to be hesitant to say what he wanted. Finally, he almost blurted out. "What I'm trying to say is that on these days, there can be no physical intimacy. Though it is no big deal, I wanted to tell you this beforehand."

The guy was forthright, if nothing else, thought Ragini, but completely unhinged. She kept quiet till they returned home. As Deepak went to his room, she hurriedly summoned a meeting of her family.

She asked them for their views. Her father was non-committal and Aman disapproved. Kamini, however, asked Ragini to compromise and look at the bigger picture of getting married and finding stability.

"Didi, does getting married means I say yes to a person whose thinking is totally incompatible with mine? For me, a second marriage is important for the sake of fulfilment, companionship and happiness. Do you think I will be getting even an iota of that with this – this toad? I'll be kneading dough, fetching milk, doing prayers, and ... and ..." Ragini barely managed to stop short of saying "performing occasional sex".

Kamini fell quiet on hearing Ragini's outburst. She looked at Aman for support. But Aman's evaluation of Deepak was no different. To their surprise, for once Ragini's father agreed with her.

"Ragini's marriage decision will have to be very carefully made. If she finds no compatibility with Deepak, we have to stand by her and not force her. I understand that she needs a companion but as she has rightly said, it needn't be a toad," he said firmly.

Decision made, the tension dissolved as they all burst into laughter, talking of Deepak's funny ways as they huddled together to discuss how to convey their refusal to Deepak's family. Ragini hoped that he himself would disapprove of the match as he had done for so many proposals earlier. However, she hoped in vain. Deepak's mother announced happily at dinner time that her son had approved of Ragini and they were ready to perform the engagement ceremony right away and then discuss the rest of the marriage arrangements.

There was an awkward silence. Ragini's father tactfully said that they wanted to do a proper function and invite the family and that meant some time would be needed. Early next morning, they arranged a sight-seeing trip for the Shrivastavs before they returned to Kanpur in the evening. Aman had a tough time conveying the no to his sister and through her to Deepak, but he ultimately succeeded.

Ragini developed fever by the evening and extended her leave. However, even while resting in bed all the time, there was no relaxing her mind. She tossed between waves of uncertainty and dilemma. Should she drop her desire of marrying again? Was she destined to be alone, to not have children? Her thoughts consumed and depressed her. The approaching autumn weather added to her melancholy and there was no solace for her in the days that followed.

*****

Of Complaints and Bollywood

When Ragini returned to Lucknow, her boss, the Deputy Manager, summoned her. She had recently finished her probation successfully and got a promotion as an Assistant Manager. She enjoyed a good reputation in the office as a professional and her boss often handed her important assignments, relying on her ability to deliver quickly and efficiently. The research cell of the bank, where she was currently posted, handled many profitable projects for the bank, generating funds and analysing data for prospective donors. In fact, Ragini was in charge of the development of the donor database and the work was confidential in nature. Ragini had an aptitude for it. More so, it gave her the weekends off as it was like back-end office work. Thinking that her boss had called her for giving another assignment, Ragini went cheerfully to his room.

But the Deputy Manager was frowning as she entered. She was shocked when she heard the reason. He had received a complaint against her. Ragini was aghast and didn't know how to respond. She could definitely do without more troubles in her life.

The complaint was about her current research project. She had recently submitted an interim report and the allegation was that it was all plagiarized. She had been accused of copying material from the internet and old research reports. The complaint gave the names of a few websites and details of old research papers as the source of her present research. It also said that she had actually not been working on her job during office hours. She had taken off from work and submitted a plagiarized report to cover up.

"There will be a strict enquiry and serious consequences if anything untoward comes out," her boss said quietly. Ragini was almost in tears.

True, she had referred to websites and old reports. But all that was going to be acknowledged in the final report. How could she prove that? Feeling distressed, she called up Mia and asked her to come over home in the evening.

As they both sipped tea in the evening, Mia started questioning Ragini. "The complaint is the work of somebody who knows you well. Who could it be?" she asked.

They could think only of Kadamb. But Ragini recalled how relievedKadamb had been that she was giving an easy divorce by mutual consent rather than slapping a notice of cruelty on him and his family. He had told her that he was very grateful to her. Moreover, the news was that he was happily married and was in a distant city. Ragini could not see any possible gain to him by stooping to act so low now.

"It has to be somebody else, maybe from your office itself," Mia thought out aloud.

Ragini wondered who it could be. She kept a low profile in office and maintained her distance from her colleagues. She believed she had no close friends or foes. So who could it be?

Then it dawned on her. Of course, it was Ashutosh Verma!

Ashutosh Verma was her colleague. He was in her team until some time ago and knew about the project. He was from Madhya Pradesh. Although boyish in looks, with a skinny body and fair complexion, most girls in the office considered him good laughter material because of his typical mannerisms and way of speaking.

He had joined the team at the time when Ragini was in the middle of her divorce and hence at a low phase emotionally. She could sense that Ashutosh had a soft corner for her but she was not inclined to respond. Neither did she like him, nor was she free from her divorce at that time.

One day she discovered a note attached to her file.

Dear Ragini-ji
I have always liked you very much. I think we will make a great team. Please consider this my proposal and say yes to marrying me.
I will try always to keep you happy.
Yours,
Ashutosh Verma

Ragini was shocked. Her mind was already in turmoil and she did not want to take any decision right then. Moreover, she did not like him. She decided to have a plain talk with him.

When they met, she told him point-blank that her divorce was not yet through and she would not consider any proposal until then. She also made it clear that she was not exactly enamoured by him. Ashutosh was also slightly younger than her, unmarried and she wasn't clear why he would want to marry her. Hence, she advised him to look elsewhere for a more suitable bride. But Ashutosh was adamant.

"I like you so much Ragini-ji that I will face all hurdles," he said. "I will deal with the society as well as my family if they oppose my decision."

Ashutosh was not ready to accept her no and soon she found him following her around her in office, getting tea and snacks for her and generally acting like her guardian. Ragini was exasperated and was wondering what to do next when the proverbial last straw happened.

Ashutosh started appearing in front of her house every morning and would follow her to office, driving behind her cab on his scooter. When she confronted him, he politely said he was not disturbing her and was merely taking that route to office. Fed up, Ragini reminded him of the HR policy in the office against harassment of women and told him that she would be forced to report his behaviour to the complaints committee. Ashutosh then stopped his nefarious stalking and even got himself transferred to another team. That was a year ago and Ragini had forgotten the episode, until now.

Yes, it must be him, agreed Mia. Ragini was certain that Ashutosh nurtured a grudge against her and had sent the complaint. The question was how to get him to admit that he had written that fictitious complaint and get him to withdraw it.

"Is he still single?" asked Mia.

"I think so," replied Ragini.

"Then let's rekindle his love for you," Mia said with a naughty look.

Ragini wasn't sure if it was a good idea but Mia insisted. This was the only way to end her troubles, she said. Mia hatched a plot to convince Ashutosh that Ragini had now fallen for him and was ready for marriage and get him to confess. She persuaded Ragini to meet Ashutosh as soon as possible.

The next day Ragini went straight to Ashutosh's desk. "Hi," she said animatedly to a totally surprised Ashutosh. Hurriedly he scrambled to his feet and tried to mumble something.

"I thought we could meet today after office and generally catch up," Ragini said, almost flirting with him, twirling her locks with one hand. Ashutosh was numb with joy.

"Sure, sure. It'll be a great pleasure Ragini-ji," he said excitedly and asked her where she wanted to meet. Ragini suggested Tea Point, a popular cafe near their office and Ashutosh readily agreed.

In the evening, over tea and samosas, Ashutosh lost no time in reiterating his proposal, saying how much he cared for her. His haste and eagerness confirmed to Ragini that he had written the complaint, foolishly hoping that it would make her turn to him. She was full of disgust at this man's vile thoughts and for the damage he had done to her.

Unaware of her thoughts, Ashutosh was being expressive of his feelings about her and was starting to reach out for her hand when Ragini remembered Mia's coaching. She stopped Ashutosh midway and insisted on going home without giving any answer to him.

She repeated the scene the next day and the day after. Ashutosh became increasingly restless and it was on the fourth "date" that Ragini upped the ante. She told Ashutosh that though she was drawn to him, her job was equally important to her.

"In fact, I'm quite ambitious and really want to rise in my career," she confided to an eagerly listening Ashutosh. "But there is a big problem. There is a complaint against me to the management. This is a hurdle in my promotion," she said and observed Ashutosh keenly as she narrated the details. As expected, Ashutosh reacted – his face went white and he could not look Ragini in the eye.

Sensing success, Ragini carried on. "I can't marry you with this sword of Damocles hanging over me. What if the enquiry goes against me? There will be ignominy for me and my family. I don't want that shadow to cloud your reputation," said Ragini, feeling very smart as she articulated an apparently logical reason for her hesitation in accepting his marriage proposal.

"Well, Ragini-ji," stuttered Ashutosh, "I fully believe in your innocence. I am sure the complaint will not hold good. Don't let it become an issue for deciding about my proposal."

But Ragini held her ground, leaving Ashutosh in a quandary. He recalled how he had plotted and planned before drafting the complaint and mailing it to the management with a pseudo name and details, waiting with a perverse pleasure for the harm that was sure to befall Ragini. After all, she had humiliated and even threatened him. She fully deserved it.

But now the changed situation had put him in a fix. Ragini appeared ready to marry him. He cursed himself. He should have simply waited for her rather than create this mess. Now what could he do? Withdrawing the false complaint was difficult. If he told the truth to the management, they would take action against him and he would lose Ragini as well. He tossed-and-turned the whole night, caught in a web of trouble of his own making.

By the morning he decided that the only thing he could do was to confess to Ragini. Ragini was such a simple girl. Surely, she would understand and forgive her future husband. This was the only way this problem could be solved. The more Ashutosh thought about it, the more convinced he was that this was the best solution. And so, as soon as he finished his breakfast of aloo parathas laden with butter, he called up Ragini.

"I have something very important to discuss. Can we meet now, before office?" he asked.

Ragini, sensing that their plan was succeeding, agreed immediately and then excitedly informed Mia. Mia repeated the instructions again. Ragini rushed off to the café and waited for Ashutosh at their usual place.

Ashutosh arrived and in his usual bumbling manner started to tell Ragini about what he had done. "Ragini-ji, please forgive me but it was I who drafted that complaint and sent it to your boss. I was very angry and hurt at the way you had treated me last year and I could not forget it. After all, I was only wanting to marry you but you insulted me by saying that you did not like me. My pride was hurt. And so I wanted to take revenge. I am very sorry, please forgive me and forget about this episode. After marriage, anyway, you don't have to work. We will go to Bhopal and I will take care of you. Please Ragini-ji, you have to understand me."

Ragini tried very hard to conceal her anger. Ashutosh's audacity was really shocking.

"Well, Ashutosh, I need time to think about all this. While I'm relieved that the complaint is fictitious, I still have to sort it out with my boss. What can I tell him?" Ragini asked.

"You just resign, Ragini-ji, and come to Bhopal, rest will be taken care of," was all Ashutosh could say.

Somehow Ragini controlled herself and managed to leave the café without losing her cool. She went straight to Mia, who had missed her office and was waiting for her.

Mia jumped with joy upon hearing that Ashutosh had confessed. "Were you able to record it?" She asked excitedly.

"I think so," said Ragini and with a big grin she brought out her phone and played the recorded conversation. Both girls listened eagerly. The recording was quite clear.

"You just resign, Ragini-ji and come to Bhopal," Mia mimicked Ashutosh to perfection.

Sharing the recording with the management was the next step. While Mia and Ragini were conscious that Ashutosh might turn more vicious after his hideous act came out, they were relying on the bank's rules against harassment of women to protect Ragini.

"And now let's celebrate," said the ever-chirpy Mia. Ragini too was in a cheerful mood and both friends set out for a movie, Ragini deciding to go to office only the next day now.

The light-hearted movie *No Entry* starred Ragini's favourite hero Anil Kapoor and was becoming a big blockbuster of the year. While it was a good distraction from her gloomy thoughts, the theme of the movie revolved around a committed marriage and at times Ragini caught herself in what she now called her "wishful thinking mode" – if only she had found a real Anil Kapoor in her life. Mia, who obviously knew about her immense liking for the suave hero, kept teasing her during the movie.

After the movie they continued their celebration, deciding to indulge in a hearty meal.

Ashutosh tried to contact her, but Ragini did not take his calls and slept peacefully at night.

The next morning Ragini marched up to her boss and made him hear the entire recording. He was full of sympathy for her. Since it was a serious matter, he took her immediately to the head of the human relations department. Ashutosh was summoned and asked to proceed on leave while an enquiry was initiated against him. He was also warned that if he tried to harass Ragini, a complaint would be filed with the police and he could very well find himself behind bars.

Ragini's boss apologized to her for not trusting her earlier. He asked her to work with full confidence and promised all support in the future. Ragini said she was happy the way things had turned out and assured him of her full commitment.

On the way back home in the evening, a sense of sadness enveloped her. Would all this have happened if she was married? How many more struggles were to come her way? She spent the journey feeling restless and by the time she reached home, she was extremely worked-up again.

She cooked herself Maggi for dinner, her thoughts still on the entire Ashutosh episode. She decided that she needed to make more concrete efforts for remarriage and so, after dinner, she determinedly dragged her laptop towards her and after many days logged into DivorceeMatrimony.com.

She saw an interesting message in her inbox with the subject line "Seeking Love".

The proposal was from Krishna who worked in the film industry in Mumbai. Not only worked but he actually sounded filmy, thought Ragini, as she read on. His photograph was displayed prominently in his profile. He was good looking in a flashy sort of way. He said he was unmarried as so far he had not met his lady-love and was looking for a mature, understanding life partner.

"Fair enough," thought Ragini, feeling rather excited at the prospect of engaging with someone from Bollywood. She was amused at her excitement but then she told herself that she was a small-town girl, after all.

She wondered why a second marriage website had profiles of so many bachelors and that made her question why Krishna, who was unmarried, would be interested in her, who had been through a divorce. Maybe divorcees appeared more keen to get married and were an easy prey for flirting. She forced herself to dismiss her negative thoughts and tried to be rational. She replied to the email cautiously and described herself a little.

Krishna responded the next day itself. Ragini liked his easy way of communication. She replied with warmth and so a good rapport was soon built between them.

They had been communicating for a week when Krishna asked for her phone number. Ragini gave it hesitantly, remembering the earlier incidents. But this time she was determined to succeed.

"Hello," she said softly when Krishna called for the first time.

"Hey Ragini, how are you doing?" Krishna's voice sounded breezy and carefree.

They talked for a long time. Krishna spoke about his Bollywood struggles, how he had come from a small town in Bihar with dreams of becoming a big star, but how instead he was now a production assistant. Ragini listened spellbound, mesmerized by his sing-song baritone and the stories he told. She was more impressed when she learned that singing was also his hobby. And before Ragini could share more about her love for Bollywood in general and Anil Kapoor in particular, Krishna broke into the all-time popular song, "My heart is beating, keeps on repeating, I'm waiting for you." Ragini laughed and didn't know what to make of it. But she was sure, she didn't mind it. Maybe she needed a lively person like Krishna to end her feeling of depression. And so, though he sounded more Mia type than hers, she continued to interact with him.

Krishna insisted she should come to Mumbai. As he passionately sang more songs to her, in the hope of finding love, she had hesitantly agreed. Once Krishna came to know about her fondness for Anil Kapoor, he used the promise of getting her to meet him as an additional bait. This thrilled Ragini further. Her distant cousin Renu lived in Mumbai and she could stay with her.

Ragini told Kamini about her plan to visit Mumbai to meet Krishna. Kamini was against the idea at first but Ragini said that going out of Lucknow and a change of scene would do her good. Kamini agreed in the end and so she made a plan to spend a weekend in Mumbai. Knowing that their father would disapprove, they did not tell him anything, though this made Kamini uncomfortable.

Ragini shared with Mia how wicked her connivance with Kamini had made her feel. But Mia also encouraged her. She had liked listening about the flamboyant Krishna. She considered going along with Ragini and almost said so, but then she thought probably Ragini wanted to go alone. She wasn't a child anymore. And so she told Ragini to go as soon as possible and helped her get the bookings done.

When the wheels of the plane touched the runway at Mumbai airport with a loud thud, Ragini found her heartbeats were making equally loud thuds. Past experiences made her feel anxious and she wondered if she had been foolish to come here. But it was too late to do anything now, so she geared up to meet Krishna. She had worn beige trousers teamed with a floral shirt and looked smart, unaware of the admiring looks of the fellow passengers.

Coming out of the airport, Ragini looked around, trying to find Krishna in the sea of faces in front of her when suddenly someone embraced her from behind and whispered "Hi" in her ears. Startled, she turned around to find herself staring into the deep brown eyes of Krishna.

"Did I startle you?" he asked with a smile. Ragini was taken in by his fair, clean-shaven good looks. His wavy and longish hair was almost golden brown. Ragini gave a silent, shy smile to Krishna, accepting his extra warm welcome.

Krishna took her bag and together they walked to the car park, Ragini liking the sense of togetherness it conveyed. "Here's my humble car," said Krishna as he flamboyantly opened the door of his red Maruti Swift for her. Ragini, now quite overwhelmed by all the attention, gladly sank in the front seat. Krishna started humming lines from another Bollywood number as the car moved in the traffic, "I want to play the game of love, I want you in the name of love." Ragini found herself blushing and she decided to strike a conversation in order to end her shyness.

She asked to be dropped to her cousin's place in Andheri. "Why, you didn't like me or what?" teased Krishna and again Ragini felt drawn towards him.

"No, no, it's not that," she replied hurriedly. "My cousin is waiting for me."

"Well, so am I," Krishna whispered gently and Ragini blushed again.

Krishna drove fast and soon brought her to the famous Mehboob studio in Bandra. It was then that Ragini realized his plan. She was going to meet her idol, Anil Kapoor! She could not believe it – a hero who she had worshipped since years was soon going to be in front of her. She felt elated and grateful to Krishna. And then the extremely fair, superbly fit Anil Kapoor was in front of them.

Ragini was mesmerized and could barely mumble how much she adored him since long.

Anil Kapoor was not only sophisticated but very polite as well. He acknowledged Krishna and then chatted merrily with Ragini, who had gathered her wits by then to be able to talk with him about her favourite movies. He made her feel extra special by giving her three autographed pictures, each with a message to her. Krishna also took her photographs with Anil Kapoor, and Ragini was on cloud nine.

Afterwards, they watched the talented star shoot for a while and then Krishna whisked her away for lunch at a fancy place nearby. Everyone there looked like a film star to Ragini. She could not contain her joy and could hardly focus on the well-presented food or for that matter even Krishna. She had just met her dream hero and she could chatter only about that. Krishna was patient and regaled her with stories about more Bollywood stars.

Ragini was still feeling elated when Krishna dropped her in front of her cousin's home. They agreed to meet in two hours at a nearby park.

Ragini's cousin, Renu, was amused at Ragini's non-stop talk of her meeting with Anil Kapoor. After some time Ragini told Renu about the real purpose of her visit. As Renu wished her luck, Ragini felt optimistic. This time things will fall in place, she thought, still upbeat after meeting her dream star. To her, arranging a meeting with Anil Kapoor had shown that Krishna cared for her. Krishna was decent, doing well in life and appeared to be in love with her. She too liked him and while his flashy ways went a little overboard at times, he appeared compatible to her in most ways.

And so, wearing in a knee-length dress, picked amid protests by Mia, Ragini looked her charming best in the evening and flirted with Krishna as he gazed at her lovingly. As she allowed Krishna to steal a kiss, Ragini felt herself aroused after a long time. Krishna hugged her tightly and told her he would've made love if he could, right there in the park. Ragini was glad that he couldn't, though she wouldn't have resisted if he had tried.

Krishna took her on a drive around Mumbai and showed her the landmarks like the Haji Ali Dargah and Gateway of India. He bought her a lovely chiffon sari as a gift and Ragini was full of joy.

"So, do I take it as a yes?" asked Krishna, squeezing her hand, drawing her close, as they walked out of the sari shop in the mall.

"Well," Ragini replied, her mischievous side coming to the fore. "When have you asked?"

Krishna immediately went down on one knee and dramatically sang another popular number, "Will you marry me?" right in the middle of the mall. Ragini burst out laughing and told him to wait for her reply.

He took Ragini to his small, rented apartment in Andheri and held her closely while continuing to kiss her. As Ragini felt herself respond to his tender yet passionate touch, Krishna became more fervent and it looked as if they would cross all barriers. But Ragini stopped herself with great difficulty and brought the conversation around to family and marriage. Krishna, as gentlemanly as ever, did not force the issue but drew back with a sigh and started talking about his family.

His parents and younger brother were still in his native town near Patna and he visited them at least once a year. His brother was studying and wanted to come to Mumbai for a job after that. His parents belonged to a very humble background and were very keen that he married a decent, well-educated girl soon. And he had found that girl in Ragini.

Ragini explained to him about her father's possible reluctance so he agreed to bring his parents to Banaras to meet Ragini's family and fix a date for marriage. He described his financial position and explained how he was now trying to get into a profit-sharing model with the producers.

Then suddenly, without any drama surprisingly, he slipped a diamond ring on Ragini's finger and holding her, announced that they were officially engaged. Ragini was ecstatic and felt secure in Krishna's arms. They cuddled together and it was late by the time she returned back to her cousin, who eyed her suspiciously. But Ragini chose to keep her engagement a secret. She thought of calling Kamini and Mia but she was so full of thoughts about Krishna that she simply lay in her bed in a daze. Krishna called her and while talking, she drifted off to a peaceful sleep. Thankfully, the planes didn't bother her that night.

The next morning Ragini texted Kamini and Mia that she was fine and would call them soon with all the details. She then informed her cousin that Krishna had proposed to her and she may soon have to attend her marriage. Renu was delighted to hear this news and immediately took her to the Siddhi Vinayak temple to thank and take blessings.

Ragini then shopped a bit and bought gifts for Mia, Kamini and her nephew. Soon it was time for her afternoon flight. Krishna had cited work issues and could not come to see her off. He said he would be working from home and had a lot of work to catch up.

On the way to the airport, Ragini remembered the effect that his kisses had on her. She wished she hadn't stopped Krishna from making love to her. She was so consumed by these thoughts and her desire that an idea formed in her mind as her cab approached the airport. She called Mia and requested her to postpone her flight and asked the cab to turn around.

Soon her cab stopped in front of Krishna's house. Mia sent a message that she had booked her on the next flight. She now had at least four hours of time – with Krishna. Krishna had called her earlier and wished her a safe flight and Ragini had confirmed that he was indeed working from home. And so she rang the doorbell with anticipation and hoped that this adventurous side of her would appeal to Krishna.

A dishevelled Krishna opened the door after she had rung the bell for quite a while. And the smile of welcome which Ragini was waiting for didn't appear on his normally cheerful face. He looked taken aback instead.

"What are you doing here? You had to catch your flight by now!" he exclaimed, not even asking her to come in. Ragini felt her joy dissipating and wondered at his inexplicable behaviour.

"Can I come in?" she finally asked and Krishna reluctantly let her into the small hall.

"Hey Krish, where are you, who is it?" asked a squeaky voice from the bedroom and Ragini decided to see for herself if what her mind was telling was true. She ran towards the bedroom and saw another dishevelled guy between the sheets. As the shock registered, she felt her new-born, happy world coming crumbling apart. How could it be true? She remembered she had come with the idea of making love and felt nauseated.

"Wait, I can explain," Krishna tried to speak, but Ragini stopped him, took off the ring and threw it at him. And then tears overtook her. The other fellow also appeared shocked and Ragini left them to sort out their mess, hearing words like "family pressure" as she came out of the apartment.

She realized she had barely been saved from a very scary future and she thanked her stars. At the same time, she felt drained due to the roller coaster ride of her emotions. She could not believe things had turned out like this. In just one day, she had seen two contrasting sides of Krishna. She knew she would find trusting anyone a difficult thing now.

With nowhere else to go, she reached the airport much before time. After the security check, she bought herself some coffee and then called Mia. With a wry smile she listened to the caller tune on Mia's phone, "I want to break free …"

*****

Kidney Beans

Ragini arrived at Lucknow where a restless night awaited her. The planes visited her again and she tossed and turned as she dreamt of planes not being able to take off and taxiing on the roads instead of runways. The next morning Ragini woke with a heavy head and gloomy thoughts which even the bright sunlight around her could not lighten.

She had talked to Kamini and Mia from the airport. Both of them had been sympathetic on phone but Ragini was not comforted. Kamini had been shocked and almost told her to stop the search for a husband now. Mia wanted to meet her as soon as she landed in Lucknow, but Ragini simply wanted to be left alone. She was distressed by thoughts of what would have happened had she actually married Krishna. And on top of that she was despaired by thoughts that she would never succeed in her endeavour to marry again. Why was it so difficult? Almost six months had passed since her divorce and while Kadamb was already married, she was struggling and failing, failing and struggling. It was not as simple as she had thought and, moreover, she was hurting herself in the process, each attempt to marry again leaving her with a scar and a broken heart.

She made tea and putting all thoughts aside, turned to the newspaper, only to find it full of news about the marriage of a celebrity couple. It was a second marriage for the actor who had divorced his first wife and found love again. Their story appeared totally out of touch with the bitter reality she was facing.

Ragini started pondering over her recent experiences. While Krishna's deceit was foremost in her thoughts and made her angry and sad at the same time, she wondered about the others she had encountered. Was she being too demanding? Could she have married any of the suitors she had met in the past few months? To what extent should she compromise to be able to get married again? Or should she totally give up the idea and get used to staying single? The constant barrage of questions made her head throb. It was only with great effort that she pushed them all away and got ready for her office.

A week passed thus, in listless monotony.

It was mid-October and Diwali was approaching. Kamini said she would feel better if she came to Banaras for the festival and urged her to come. After some persuasion, Ragini agreed.

At Banaras, Ragini put up the Diwali lights along with young Shrey. The activity released some of her tension. Kamini and Aman were very supportive and even her father appeared to be more caring. She did not discuss her marriage and distracted herself by going out or spending time with Shrey. Kamini did remark once that she should not be too adventurous and be very clear about what she was seeking in a life partner. She told her to think about her priorities and then seek a companion. Ragini knew what she meant. She should not go after every random person she encountered on the internet. Feeling wiser and comforted, she returned to Lucknow in a better frame of mind.

As she unpacked, she went through her criteria for an ideal match she had made in her mind and could not weed out anything from the list at all. She wanted education, a kind heart, a decent profession and a like-minded family, that was all. Was that too much? Good looks were a bonus, she believed. She wanted only the basic essentials of a good human being in a life partner, so she was sure wasn't over-expecting. It was merely bad luck that she had come across the wrong types so far, she consoled herself.

And then the point struck her – she was simply answering the messages that came to her inbox. She was not searching the profiles on her own. That's why Mr Right had not been found yet. Excited by her newfound enlightenment, she dropped everything, opened the laptop, ignored her inbox and started browsing. The list of prospects was huge. Shortlisting itself was a task. She again focused on her parameters to eliminate as many as possible from the profiles in front of her.

Finally, she came across a profile that appeared suitable.

Ravish Mitra was an attractive 33-year-old, from Kolkata, working as a journalist with a prominent newspaper in New Delhi. He was recently divorced and lived with his five-year-old daughter in his own home in South Delhi. His profile seemed to meet Ragini's parameters. The only trouble was that he was looking for a non-working woman to share his life with. However, Ragini decided to try her luck. She sent him an email with her details, expressing interest in his profile.

A week passed but there was no response. Not liking the "rejection", Ragini decided to do what Mia had been telling her to do for many days – become a paid member of the website so that she could get direct access to the contact details of the profiles she liked. She paid the membership charges and brushing aside the welcome emails from the website, she accessed Ravish Mitra's phone number and without further ado, dialled him.

A sharp voice answered. Ragini was taken aback for a second by her own cheek in making the call and the brusque response, but then gathered her wits and began.

"Hello, I'm Ragini Mathur. I sent you a message expressing interest in your profile at DivorceeMatrimony.com. I called up to confirm whether you have received it."

There was silence for a moment on the other end and then Ravish said, "Ms Ragini, I don't remember seeing your message. But I don't visit the website too frequently. I will have a look and then get back to you."

He sounded curt but Ragini persisted. "Now that I've called, maybe we can chat and exchange notes for a while," she said.

"Ms Ragini, this is not a convenient time for me. I have work to attend to and I've to take care of my little daughter. Perhaps we can talk tomorrow during the day time."

Ragini realized then that it was 9 p.m. and her impulsive step was making her look rather foolish and even desperate. Saying that she could not talk during office hours, she hung up hurriedly and regretted making the call.

She tried to search more profiles but didn't find anything worthwhile. And so picking up a recent bestseller by Danielle Steel where the protagonist succeeds in getting the man of her dreams to marry her, Ragini tried to fall asleep with similar thoughts.

"Wow, Ragini, you are really aggressive!" exclaimed Kamini upon hearing her recent escapade. "Very unlike what you have been so far," she added.

Ragini kept quiet as a slight depression was beginning to overtake her. She was tired of all thoughts about marriage but sadly these were her only thoughts all the time. Each failed effort at remarriage was reinforcing rejection in her. She thought she was coming to a point where she had to accept that a second marriage was not going to happen. Well, at least her father would be happy, she thought. Sensing her despair, Kamini decided to make more efforts to find a match for her.

Over the weekend, as the sun shone bright in the October sky, Ragini's mood changed, but the reason had nothing to do with the weather. She received an email from Ravish Mitra – so she hadn't been rejected, after all.

Dear Ms Ragini,

I have finally seen your email and also your profile. Other than the fact that you are working, I do not find any reason not to take your proposal further. I have a real issue with working women due to the sour experience in my previous marriage. Suffice to say, it is a very important requirement for me and unless you are willing to accept this, it is futile to interact further.

Yours truly,

Ravish

Now that was some food for thought, Ragini thought, happy at receiving at least a response from Ravish. He sounded very clear about what he wanted and that was always a good sign. She asked Mia to come over and both got into an animated discussion about Ravish.

Mia was dismissive about the proposal. Wanting a non-working wife made him rather regressive, she argued.

"It is not a good precondition," she said firmly. "Whether you work or not should be entirely your decision. Nobody should impose conditions about it."

While Ragini agreed with Mia, she said they should consider Ravish's situation also.

"He says he is speaking from his previous sour experience. That cannot be denied. After all, I also would not ever want to face any cruelty or abuse again," said Ragini with understanding.

However, Mia was not convinced and told Ragini to look for another proposal, but Ragini did not agree. Mia reminded her of her unwillingness to leave her job for Prabhat in US, but Ragini insisted that the situation was different here. Besides, she was getting tired of searching and things not working out. It was frustrating. She decided to email Ravish.

Dear Ravish,

Thank you for your email. It is good to know that you have clarity about your requirements for a life partner. I too have certain parameters which I thought may be met by you and hence I'd shown the interest in your profile. I'm looking for a life partner who believes in equality between men and women, who is gentle, caring and generous and is well-settled in life. Since I also had a bitter experience in my previous marriage, any form of aggression is totally unacceptable to me. It is important you accept that, if we have to go any further.

As far as your condition of a non-working wife is concerned, while I believe that having financial security and independence is a pre-requisite in today's times where tolerance among individuals is dropping alarmingly, leading to more break-ups than ever, yet understanding and respecting your requirement, I would not be rigid about leaving my job post-marriage.

Hope that suffices for now. I would like to understand your thoughts on this issue a bit more so that I can make a correct decision.

If you want, we can continue interacting on emails; otherwise you have my phone number.

Regards,

Ragini

Ragini felt good and rather calm as she sent the email and waited for a response. Maybe this would be the last time she would need to search for a partner.

The response came quickly indeed. It was brief.

Hello Ragini,

I'm quite impressed by your rational thinking. I have always wanted an intellectual life partner who can be my equal in all things. I am not aggressive by nature and abhor violence of any kind to anyone, so you can rest assured on that. I will be calling you soon so that we can exchange more views.

Regards,

Ravish

Ragini was filled with joy. At last there was some positive development. She was happy that she hadn't paid heed to Mia and happily narrated the entire details to Kamini. Kamini was relieved to find Ragini happy and out of the sorrowful state she had got into. She prayed for things to turn out well. Mia was quiet when she came to know of the developments, but Ragini continued being exhilarated.

And so Ravish found a very cheerful, playful Ragini when he called up after two days. They exchanged pleasantries and as Ravish got talking,

Ragini found him quite vociferous about his likes and dislikes.

"I've had a very bitter experience. My ex-wife cheated on me and left me for a colleague of hers. Not only me, she heartlessly left our child – what more can I say? I gave all the liberty to her and trusted her completely. Ours was a love-marriage. I knew her since college. I let her do what she wanted in life and look where it has left me. So I'm very clear that now my wife has to listen to and follow certain things that I want."

Ragini asked very quietly, "You will not let your wife do anything what she wants to do? Don't you think that's unfair?"

"I'm not asking you to marry me if you think it's unfair," came the caustic, offensive reply and Ragini became quiet.

"Listen Ragini," Ravish continued, "I'm not a monster who will keep his wife in a cage. But I'm very clear about what I expect from my life partner. And I'm talking to you only because you wrote that you will leave your job if this works out. I want a mother for my daughter, not a part-time machine who is torn between home and office," Ravish's tone became pungent again.

Ragini was puzzled. Why did he turn so bitter? Why was he so volatile? She also had a traumatic past but she was not letting it interfere in her life. Ravish was not even giving her a chance to speak. She tried to focus her mind on what Ravish was now saying.

"That woman, she misused her freedom. I did not suspect anything. I'm basically a trusting person plus my work keeps me very busy. "Ravish was still going on about his ex-wife. "She just came home one day and declared that she was going to leave me. It was such a shock. How could she be so callous? She didn't even think of what will happen to her own daughter. What kind of a person does that?"

Tired of this tirade, Ragini cut in between and told Ravish that probably his daughter was crying in the background. Ravish grumbled about the irresponsible attitude of the maid for a few seconds before finally keeping the phone down.

"Phew!" thought Ragini. Almost an hour-long talk and they had not got anywhere. Damn his ex-wife, was all that Ragini could think of as she drifted off to sleep.

Ragini called Ravish the next day but he didn't pick up the phone. He sent a message that he would call her after dinner. Ragini was beginning to dislike his dominating and self-centred attitude. However, she was determined to try her best and not let the opportunity fizzle out.

It was late in the night when Ravish called. Ragini answered sleepily, but became alert when she heard what he was saying.

"I'm having second thoughts. What if things don't turn out fine? My daughter will be the person most affected. Can you guarantee me that you will make the marriage work?"

"Ravish, I alone cannot make it work. Both of us will have to work towards it. Both have to adapt and adjust."

But Ravish was not convinced. He was in a different frame of mind altogether. He went on talking negatively.

"What if you also ditch me or just try to live on your own terms? I will not be able to cope with that."

Ragini tried her best to remove his doubts but Ravish was turning out to be a very complicated person. In order to lighten the atmosphere, she decided to tease him a bit.

"Look, we are not getting married tomorrow. I'm not wearing a bridal dress nor asking you to wear a sherwani and come galloping on a horse to marry me now."

"No, no, no!" Ravish almost screamed. "What are you saying? All this scares me. I am not up to it." And with that he abruptly disconnected the phone.

Her playfulness had boomeranged. Ragini was also upset by how Ravish had behaved and called up Mia. Mia was on a short trip to Rishikesh with her office colleagues. In times like these, Ragini envied her carefree attitude. Mia had asked her to come for the trip, too, but Ragini had been so caught up in the interactions with Ravish that she could not focus on anything else. Mia was outraged when she heard what had happened. She told Ragini to have a final talk with Ravish – if at all he called back.

Ravish called up in the morning and apologized for what he said the previous night.

"My anxieties of the past got the better of me," he confessed. "I'm working on them and with time they will be resolved. If you are still willing to talk to me and take things further, we can discuss a few more things like food habits, my daughter and whether we will have more children."

Recalling Mia's advice, Ragini decided to settle matters once and for all.

"So let's talk about food habits," she said, only half-hearing what Ravish had been saying and focussing on the least significant of the issues Ravish had mentioned.

"I love fish in non-vegetarian food, so I hope you know how to cook it," Ravish started.

Ragini was a vegetarian. Though she knew how to cook chicken, but fish? Before she could answer, Ravish went on.

"Even if you don't know how to cook it, you will have to learn because it's so important to me. And one more thing. Kidney beans are banned from my house because my ex-wife loved them and made them often. I hate the sight of it now."

Ragini could not believe what she was hearing. In her astonishment, she blurted, "You mean, rajma?"

"Yes, yes," answered Ravish vehemently.

By now, the sheer arrogance and the imposing attitude were too much for Ragini, who coincidentally had a weakness for rajma. And weakness or not, the man was proving himself to beyond all limits of reason and logic.

"Listen, Mr Mitra," Ragini finally burst out, "I've had enough. You are a self-centred, commitment phobic, unreasonable oaf and you certainly do not deserve me. And I would certainly prefer rajma over a nincompoop like you!"

With that Ragini banged the phone down and stormed out of the room. She went to the kitchen and with a vehemence took out rajma from the jar for preparing it in the evening, her usual calm disposition shaken by the irrational Ravish. How could a person who appeared so perfectly normal be so illogical in reality? Perhaps he was just a misogamist and throwing up these issues was his way of making excuses and staying away from marriage.

"Whatever," mumbled a still upset Ragini and turned to organize her already neat cupboard.

*****

Two White Patches

Kamini found the whole episode with Ravish silly and she was relieved to see that Ragini also thought so. Meanwhile, Kamini had been able to identify a match for Ragini and she decided to visit her to discuss the details. Ragini was delighted with this unexpected visit, more so because Shrey had also come along.

Stirring her soup, as they settled for a light dinner, Kamini started the conversation with a smile.

"Ragini, I have some news for you. Seeing you so heartbroken after you returned from Mumbai, I'd decided to intensify my efforts in finding you a match."

"Oh no," said Ragini, dramatically rolling her eyes and both sisters burst out laughing as they recalled the pompous Deepak Shrivastav.

"Let's hope this time it's different and more suitable," said Kamini optimistically as she gave details of Rajiv Asthana, brought into their lives through the most active match making efforts of Indian relatives.

Rajiv was the cousin of Aman's uncle's friend and belonged to Jaipur, Rajasthan. He was heading operations of a solar-power plant. He was 32 years old and unmarried. The photo dutifully provided by Kamini showed he was not bad looking. He looked younger than his age, had striking features and thick, black hair. He had two white patches beneath his eyes which made Ragini a little apprehensive. But Kamini was quite keen on making this marriage happen, so she told Ragini to focus on more important things.

"Look at all your requirements first," Kamini advised her younger sister.

"But why is he still unmarried?" asked Ragini.

"Apparently because he didn't find a suitable girl, which for him is a mix of tradition and modernity," replied Kamini. "You needn't worry. We are going to take the initiative this time. Both Aman and I will go to Jaipur, meet him and try to find out more details. If you want, you can come with us," continued Kamini.

Though Ragini was sceptical, she found herself agreeing with her sister. The thought of visiting the beautiful pink city was tempting. Kamini confirmed the programme to her husband and asked him to make the travel arrangements from Lucknow so that they could travel together. She spoke to her father and told him about the marriage proposal. Ragini was surprised at this bold and proactive side of her sister's personality as she, even though younger, had always been the more enterprising of the two. Kamini had always been happy to follow her lead. Ragini also felt pangs of guilt at what her family was going through because of her. Kamini, sensing her feelings, tried to put her at ease, and they decided to treat Shrey to the new animated movie *Hanuman*, followed by dinner. Mia also joined them. Mia regaled them with anecdotes from her Rishikesh trip. She had also played cupid to a budding romance between two of her colleagues and was feeling happy about it.

Ragini applied for leave from office and packed up quickly. Aman arrived the next day and they left for Jaipur.

The charming ambience of Jaipur appeared soothing to Ragini as they checked into their hotel on the beautiful JLN road. They rang up the Asthanas and reconfirmed their meeting the next day. Then they walked along the broad road and visited the pristine Birla temple, an architectural marvel in white marble. Ragini found herself praying for marital happiness and felt positive vibes enveloping her as she settled for the night.

The Asthanas lived in Police Lines. It took some time for Aman, Kamini, Ragini and Shrey to find the house. They were surprised to see that it was a small, one-bedroom government flat. Though it was below their expectations, there was nothing they could do about it.

Mrs Asthana, Rajiv's mother, welcomed them at the door. She was a polite lady but appeared uninvolved and disinterested in the whole matter. Maybe that's her nature, Ragini thought.

Rajiv soon joined them. He was a decent, warm and courteous person. He explained how, after his father, an inspector in the state police, had died suddenly due to a cardiac arrest, he had the responsibility of the whole family. His mother had still not recovered completely from the shock. They had continued to live in the same house since his mother had many memories linked to the place and he didn't want to disturb her any further. But now they were going to move out. Rajiv had already identified a two-bedroom flat in the posh Vaishali Nagar, which he intended to take on rent. Finalizing his marriage would also provide the necessary impetus to move out.

Aman talked to Rajiv about his job. Rajiv explained how he handled operations and how his job entailed travelling into the interiors of Rajasthan to towns like Phalodi and Jaisalmer, leaving his mother alone here. That was another reason for continuing to stay there because it was much safer than any other place. Aman seemed impressed with Rajiv and nudged Kamini to initiate the talk about marriage.

Kamini asked Rajiv what he was looking for in a life partner. Rajiv said he wanted a girl who could balance tradition and modernity. It was proving to be inordinately difficult.

Ragini had been a silent observer so far. She felt she could relate to Rajiv. She knew how difficult it was to find a suitable life partner. She liked the fact that Rajiv was following the norms of arranged marriage and not insisting on "dating" her. They talked for a while and both had a sense of comfort in each other's way of thinking and expectations.

The famous Jaipur snacks of pyaz kachori and jalebi were soon served and then it was time to take leave. Mrs Asthana showed some interest in the conversation finally and said they would tell them their decision soon. Kamini was okay with that as she also had to speak with their father before finalizing anything.

Rajiv suggested they could visit the historic places like the Hawa Mahal and Amber Fort before they left Jaipur. And so they spent the rest of the day sight-seeing. Ragini wished that Rajiv could have come with them but Rajiv had to travel for work.

In her happy state, Ragini was enthralled by the sights Jaipur had to offer. It was early November and the weather was pleasant, with winter just around the corner. She felt like a princess when they climbed up the Hawa Mahal. The strong breeze around them from the many windows made for the queens of Jaipur made it a little chilly. The light effects at Sheesh Mahal at the Amber Fort left them fascinated. As the valour of the Rajputana princes came alive in the fort, they were transported back into history.

In the market, she and Kamini purchased bright Bandhni outfits and lac bangles from the local shops. Ragini felt even more upbeat, due to the vibrant colours surrounding her. Shrey was happy with his shopping of colourful puppets. Kamini and Aman both seemed satisfied with the visit and so it was a cheerful family that headed back to Lucknow.

They discussed their visit on their way back. Everyone agreed that it was a good proposal and they should concur once Rajiv said yes. Of course, they had to share all the details with their father and get his approval as well. That responsibility fell on Kamini. Ragini started thinking how she would get a transfer to the Jaipur branch of her bank.

Kamini, Aman and Shrey left for Banaras from Lucknow station itself. Ragini continued to be in a dream – spellbound, like a princess awaiting her Prince Charming.

A week passed but there was no word from the Asthanas. Her father, who had given a go-ahead, was also now waiting for things to move forward. Aman called Rajiv but he did not pick up the phone. Ragini had a sense of foreboding but Kamini told her not to be pessimistic. They called up a few times again, but there was no response, no call back. Aman called his uncle's friend who had given the reference and asked him to find out what was wrong, but even his calls went unanswered. They were baffled by this strange, unexpected turn of events.

Ragini felt depressed again but decided to shrug off the incident as yet another episode in her life journey. Maybe she should really adopt Mia's attitude and look out more for a friend and companion rather than a husband, she thought listlessly as she combed her hair and got ready for office. Just then her phone rang. Ragini was surprised to find a strange female voice on the other side.

"Hello, is that Ragini Mathur?"

"Yes, who is this?"

"I'm Sheila Roy, fiancée of Rajiv Asthana."

"What?" A bewildered Ragini felt her world crumbling around her. How was that possible? They had met only around ten days ago and discussed marriage. Rajiv couldn't have finalized another proposal so soon, without telling them.

Quickly, she took hold of herself and listened carefully to what Sheila was saying.

"Did you know Rajiv was divorced?" asked Sheila.

Now what was this? Another bombshell? Ragini decided to take the lead in unravelling the story of Mr Asthana.

"Wait a minute, let's start at the beginning," said Ragini. "If you are his fiancée, why are you calling me and telling me all this? How did you get my number?"

"See Ragini, I got engaged to him two weeks ago."

This confused Ragini still more. That would be three or four days before Ragini and her family had gone and met him at his home.

"I had met Rajiv some months ago through a common friend and we were seeing each other," continued Sheila. "We got engaged two weeks ago in a simple ceremony and we are to wed in a couple of months. However, his mother told me only yesterday that he was divorced some time ago. She also mentioned about your visit to their home. She implied that you did not know he was divorced earlier. When I confronted Rajiv, he had no answers. He said he couldn't say no to your visit as a relative had insisted on it. He had thought he would call up later and convey a refusal, but had felt awkward and just kept silent, hoping you will get the hint."

And left me completely high-and-dry, fumed Ragini. Then she had another thought. "How do I know you are telling the truth?" she asked.

"That's for you to decide. Rajiv would have called back after your phone calls if he was serious, wouldn't he? And yes, you can also search the local Jaipur newspaper online. There was some news report about his divorce some time ago."

Ragini decided Sheila must be telling the truth. She immediately called up Kamini who was also astounded at hearing all this. Aman too was shocked. Rajiv could have simply told them that he had got engaged rather than carrying out such a farce. And how could he have hidden the fact that he was divorced earlier? "The man was a total fraud and ought to be put behind bars," he said. They all tried to soothe Ragini who was by now feeling traumatized and let down. But what could they do?

Ragini decided to stop her futile search where each time she was tossed around and she ended up paying a heavy price emotionally merely for believing what people said. She would be like Mia from now on and have fun with friends instead. No more chasing the Holy Grail. She would settle for what was in her destiny and accept it wholeheartedly.

She decided to take a break from her laptop and all matrimonial searches, simply take each day as it came for a while. *Que sera sera.*

*****

You don't have to understand it,
You just have to have faith.

Serendipity

You Only Live Once

Go Goa! Mia literally shouted with excitement as she entered Ragini's home one evening. Mia had welcomed her decision to stop her search and was leaving no stone unturned in assuring Ragini that life would be more fun if she continued on her resolve. So when she received her annual holiday tickets from her office, she made a plan to go to Goa with Ragini and paint the town red. Ragini found her excitement contagious and both started planning the vacation.

Azure skies welcomed them to Goa and the bright sunshine instantly cleared Ragini's mind. Mia was also her usual joyous self and they checked into a small resort right next to Miramar beach. Mia had made Ragini buy skirts and shorts for the holiday and Ragini felt good in her new clothes. They rushed to the beach and jumped into the cold but pleasant sea and then spent the whole afternoon sunbathing. Mia enjoyed a beer while Ragini settled for a cola.

"Before this holiday ends, I'll make sure you have tasted wine, beer, cocktails – everything!" Mia said passionately as Ragini laughed.

Her distaste for alcohol had always been surprising to Mia and even Ragini did not know how she had developed this dislike. Maybe her upbringing had been so strong and conventional that even Mia's insistence was not able to break it. Ragini's mind again went back to her childhood and she remembered her father's strictness and how her mother tried to balance it with her easy-going nature. Mia dragged her thoughts back to the present as she spotted a handsome man in his thirties walk past by them and ogled at him. Ragini decided it was time to head back to the resort and spent the rest of the evening watching the cultural show being put up there. They decided to have Chinese for dinner and both ate till they thought they would burst.

The next morning they decided to visit Aguada Fort, which reminded Ragini immediately of the iconic movies shot there including *Dil Chahta Hai*. At the Dona Paula beach they were fascinated as they heard a local guide narrate the various legends of Dona Paula. Love indeed makes the world go around, thought Ragini in wonder.

As they went beach-hopping, Ragini felt the sound of the waves of the ocean calmed her tempestuous thoughts giving her mind some tranquillity. She could live alone happily, she thought. There was no problem. The serene atmosphere of Basilica of Bom Jesus further strengthened her sense of peace and she sighed with pleasure as they marvelled at the architecture of the grand church.

South Goa was their target the next day and they spent a lazy day at the Colva beach and at the Palolem beach. They watched the sunset, mesmerized by the changing shades of the horizon. Mia offered Ragini a sip of her beer but Ragini wasn't tempted. Her guilty indulgence were the calorie-loaded cashews that Goa offered in abundance and for once she felt contented with life.

All too soon, it was the last day of the trip. They had a relaxed and delicious breakfast at the resort, Mia chiding her for not experimenting with Goan dishes. Ragini compensated by indulging in the delicious bebinca – the soft layered Goan dessert.

They roamed around in the local market nearby for a while and Ragini picked up a multi coloured skirt for Kamini, though she was not sure if she would wear it. They had saved the best part of the trip for the last and as the evening drew closer, they dressed up smartly in bright skirts for the cruise on River Mandovi, which promised to be an exhilarating experience. The cruise included a song-and-dance performance. The boat was crowded, brimming with enthusiastic tourists. Mia somehow found two seats in the front row for them.

The cultural programme started with a dance accompanied by Goan songs. Ragini's eyes focused on the lead dancer, who was not only a great dancer but also strikingly handsome. Neil Ribeiro was his name and he seemed to have sensed Ragini's admiration. Ragini found herself blushing as he blew flying kisses at her while dancing. A lot of girls, including Mia, were also vying for his attention but he had eyes for only Ragini.

As his dance got over and there was a break, Neil approached Ragini with a glass of red wine in his hands and introduced himself. Ragini was thrilled and chatted merrily with him. He offered the wine to Ragini and Mia couldn't believe her eyes when she saw Ragini accepting it. He stayed for a while and then left for his final dance.

Ragini looked around. It was a magical scene – lights falling softly on the water, the energetic dancers, the handsome Neil, the peppy music, the gentle movement of the boat, happy people enjoying the memorable moments. And then she looked at the glass of wine in her hands. She had taken it, not wanting Neil to think of her as an unsophisticated girl and thinking she would pass it on to Mia. But she realized she had been happily taking sips from it. The wine was mildly sweet and she quite liked the taste. Her head was spinning a little, but in a pleasant manner.

Suddenly, she wanted to feel what being intoxicated was like, to let the moment prevail and to shut out every disturbing thought from her hyperactive mind. She drank the rest of the wine in the glass in one gulp, paying no heed to Mia's advice to sip the wine slowly. She asked Mia to get her another glass and sat down to watch Neil's final performance.

As Neil began dancing, Ragini felt the wine hitting her and she felt a little dizzy. But the feeling soon settled down to a pleasant mood and she cheered Neil heartily. Neil responded by pulling her up for a dance and her protests were drowned in the loud clapping of the crowd. Neil made her dance and held her close, quite close. She felt herself tingling all over as he squeezed her and sang the lyrics to her. She followed his foot movements and tried valiantly to match his speed. As he whirled her around, he again repeated the song, "Let go, just let go of whatever pain you are holding inside you ... you only live once, listen to your heart and don't hold back, do what your heart tells you to do... remember you only live once." With that he gently escorted Ragini to her seat and went behind the curtains as the programme ended.

Both Mia and Ragini went backstage and tried to look for him but he had disappeared. Both felt despondent.

Mia took a still high Ragini to the resort and Ragini insisted on having more wine. As she drank, she let out her feelings of frustration and then started crying.

"You know Mia," she said between sobs, "all I want is to marry again. Just a simple man. I don't have many expectations. Why is it so difficult to find such a person? Is there a problem with me?"

Mia consoled her. "No problem with you, Ragini. Your approach is correct. Sooner or later you will find your man. It's my way of life which is problematic," said Mia and then became quiet. Ragini was intrigued.

As she sipped her wine and stopped Ragini from having more, Mia narrated her latest misadventure. She had met a young man through a friend of someone she was dating for a short while. Ravi Sharma was handsome and rich. His father was a millionaire and Ravi was the heir apparent to the business empire. Ravi and Mia had hit off well, meeting often and soon they became passionate lovers. After a long time Mia had felt she was going steady and she liked the feeling. She remembered the Samir incident and though her intuition told her to not get attached to Ravi, she could not stop her strong feelings. She told herself that Ravi was unlike Samir and was sure he also felt the same about her. She was certain she wanted to marry him. She refrained from telling Ragini, thinking that in the phase Ragini was, she would feel betrayed and she did not want to hurt her dear friend.

Ravi spoiled her with gifts and seemed to want her immensely. Mia expected Ravi to propose to her but Ravi, amid all his claims of love forever, showed no sign of any commitment.

One night, after a steamy lovemaking session, the frank and bold Mia herself broached the subject. Holding Ravi close to her, she asked him what he felt about marriage.

Ravi reacted violently, pushing her away saying, "We clearly agreed this was only for fun. No commitments. You can't get serious now. A fling is a fling. Anyway, I'm going abroad for a business course. To greener pastures."

Mia was heartbroken. Ravi had dismissed her cruelly, without even a thought. Mia had not been able to recover from her utter misery. Samir and

Ravi merged to form a dark nightmare for her. She was still nursing her broken heart and back to telling herself again that there was no need to find a companion who would be with her through thick-and-thin. Her single-and-mingle approach was better and would last a lifetime.

Even in her drunken state, Ragini was aghast that her friend had undergone so much and had not shared it with her. As she felt Mia's trauma, she was full of remorse about how self-centred she had been in not even noticing that Mia was depressed. Both friends burst into tears as they hugged each other. Amid the tears, Mia picked up the bottle of wine and both of them finished it before finally going off to sleep, while mumbling in their drunken stupor, "You only live once, you only live once."

Morning saw both of them in a sombre mood, Ragini feeling guilty about not being caring towards Mia and about her drunken scene and Mia feeling completely drained out emotionally.

Mia being Mia, was soon back to planning about how to get Ragini married. She knew her friend was far more emotional than her. While she had almost forgotten Ravi and was, in her mind at least, more-or-less back to her lifestyle of having fun, Ragini felt emotionally depleted with each failed endeavour to find a husband.

Their flight back to Lucknow was on time. As the plane soared, their spirits also lifted. Mia, who anyway could not stay serious for long, declared the trip to be most successful and said Neil should be thanked for introducing Ragini to wine. Ragini blushed at the memory of that dance, but felt rejuvenated and sensed her old determination to find a suitable husband coming back.

*****

Prince Charming

Returning home to Lucknow, the girls got back into their routine and Ragini was soon logging into DivorceeMatrimony.com with enthusiasm.

One evening she came across an interesting post.

> Looking for that second chance, which hopefully is the last one. Looking for that special someone who is as comfortable sitting beside me driving at 150 kmph as sitting in a park, a person with whom I can talk about everything in the world and yet enjoy the silences too. Life isn't a bed of roses but with that someone special, it needn't be a bed of thorns either.

Ragini could not help being impressed by the sincerity and the feelings in these words. She could relate to them right away. It was the profile of a person called Mani28 and was repeatedly coming up in her inbox. As she found herself drawn to the poetic words, she wondered what he looked like. She conjectured an image of a sensitive person, seeking love and companionship like her. She hoped things would work out this time, but remembered her many endeavours in the past. She was in a dilemma whether to proceed. But a small voice inside told her there was no harm in trying just one last time. The small voice grew in its insistence and Ragini found it difficult to ignore.

She also remembered Neil and his song – You only live once, listen to your heart and don't hold back – and finally decided to respond in a very factual, emotionless manner and await the result.

She emailed back:

Hi Mani28,
Saw your profile and liked it. Please go through mine and let me know if it interests you.
Ragini

She almost clicked the send button but then thought – here was the most well-written and suitable profile she'd come across so far and she was replying in such a staid manner. Impulsively, she decided to add one more line:

Maybe it's me you are looking for!

And with that as the opening line, she sent her response, told herself to take it easy and wait to find out more about Mani28 – whether Mani28 was Mani Shankar Subramaniam or Mani Bhushan Pandey or even Mani Ratnam!

The next day she updated Mia, who had expected that something like this would be happening soon. Mia cautioned her and told her to be careful. Ragini brushed aside her fears. Ever since their Goa holiday, she had become sure that she would find a loving marriage – a marriage which would take away her loneliness and erase her past wounds. And so she waited for the response from Mani28.

Sure enough, she soon got a simple reply from Mani28, expressing his desire to know more about her.

Ragini again replied matter-of-factly.

I belong to Banaras and am presently working in Lucknow. I have been through a divorce (more about that later) and am looking to remarry. My father is a retired professor and I have an elder sister who is settled in Banaras. After my mother passed away, she has been the one who has stood by me. My father also lives with her at present.

I would describe myself as a person who is simple at heart and honest in thinking. I like to live life to its fullest. At the same time one has to fulfil one's responsibilities. This balancing is what makes life's journey interesting. As I wrote in my profile, I'm looking for a life partner who is generous in mind and heart – simple words but if you can understand their profundity, then probably you are the one for me.

Do tell about yourself.

Ragini

The reply came almost immediately.

Hi Ragini,

Good to hear from you. Your response caught my attention when you wrote that maybe you are the one I'm looking for. It showed to me that you have not only read my profile thoroughly but also understood my need for an anchor, a life partner in the truest meaning of the word, which in itself is significant.

About me. My name is Mani Ratan Tiwari (Mani to friends), am 28 years old, born in Delhi, school and college from Delhi also. I did my MBA from Bangalore and am currently working in an MNC there. That is the history, so to say:-)

Like Shah Rukh Khan, I try not to be santusht with life – thoda wish karta hoon ;-). I am a thoroughbred

Gemini with multiple interests – reading, movies, music, dancing and outings with friends. I can't stand dirty kitchens or bathrooms, but my cupboard is usually a mess. Well, with fun comes responsibility too (reminds you of Spiderman☺), no doubt, and a balance between them surely makes life meaningful.
More later.
Take care.
Mani

Ragini was almost ecstatic with joy to get a positive reply from Mani28 – and one which made him appear normal and like-minded. So while Mani Ratan Tiwari hadn't mentioned what he was doing on DivorceeMatrimony.com, Ragini was enthused by the well-written response which conveyed an honest personality with a sense of humour – both appealed to Ragini a lot. There was much to be learnt still, as Mani had not even put his photo in his profile.

In a happy mood, Ragini immediately sat down to reply.

Hi Mani,
Good to hear from you. I did my college from Banaras and after my MBA I have been working in the State Bank for Rural Development in Lucknow for the past three years. I also enjoy reading, seeing movies and outings, but Lucknow as you know, is not as big a city as Bangalore for a happening social life so *Yeh dil maange more.*
I'm a typical Aquarian – rebel at heart and stubborn at times. Don't say I didn't warn you! But then, it is also a fact that Gemini and Aquarians gel well together ☺ and that's a welcome sign.

Can we exchange photos so as to know whom we are talking to?
Bye for now.

Ragini

The reply came the next day.

Hey,
Nice to know an Aquarian who is a banker. I'm sure you bring firm decision making to your work as well. I'm currently working with MV Finance as Manager and enjoy my work immensely. It's a challenging area. I am sending my photo – maybe not too good, but that's all I have. Have a look.
Bye.

Mani

Ragini didn't realize it earlier, but it struck her that presentable looks were a part of her parameters and a starting point in her match making efforts. Mani had a fair complexion with pleasant features and straight hair falling all over the forehead. He had a smiling face. She found Mani reasonably good looking and felt that it was all right to move to the next stage now – of talking to him and finding out more details.

So she wrote:

Hi Mani,
It's drizzling here today and the perfect time for Adnan Sami and hot pakodas. As I said, I work in the SDRB. I am an Assistant Manager. I look after the research cell, where I focus on market surveys and research analytics for development of databases. Though the work culture here is a little like the private sector, it is a state-run body and hence the work pressures are like any other government office.

> Your photo is nice. I'm also sending a few photographs of mine. If you like them, maybe we can talk over phone.
> Bye for now.
> Ragini

Ragini waited for a couple of days but there was no response. She grew anxious. The messages had been prompt earlier. It was surprising that after sending her photos there was silence. In that edgy mood, she sent a rather blunt email.

> If you did not like the photographs, please say so directly. That would be better than just staying silent.

In response, she got his phone number.

Hmmm, she thought, Mr Tiwari is certainly smart. Nonetheless, there was no denying that Ragini wanted to make that call and take things forward. Which she did.

Over phone Mani sounded warm and receptive. He listened to Ragini as she spoke about her first marriage and empathized with her when she talked about the violence part. He appeared in sync with her thoughts and seemed to be the much-awaited ideal suitor to Ragini.

Mani spoke about his family, which was based in Delhi – his parents, elder brother and younger sister. Wanting the suspense about his marital status to be over, Ragini then asked about the most crucial question.

"Were you married?" she asked.

"As a matter of fact, I still am," said Mani.

Ragini felt her heart sinking as she heard Mani's reply. In fact, she couldn't believe her ears. What exactly did he mean by that? Was this yet another dead-end?

"What do you mean?" she asked aggressively.

Mani explained how he was separated from his wife since the last two years and was now about to commence the divorce proceedings as reconciliation was no longer possible. He was too drained emotionally to keep making one-sided efforts.

Ragini was dismayed. After getting along so well, it was very disheartening to find that he was not divorced and not free legally to marry again. Why had he put up his profile then? Ragini shuddered involuntarily at the thought of dealing with another fraud.

Sensing her dismay, instead of getting into long explanations, Mani gently told her to take it easy and kept the phone down, saying that he would call again. Ragini liked his sensitivity but then thought, what was the point of it? Even if he started the divorce proceedings soon, it was bound to take at least a year, if not longer. And who knows, the estranged wife may not agree for a simple, mutual divorce. It may become a long-drawn battle.

As Ragini's thoughts went into a loop, her head felt heavy and she decided she needed a cup of tea – and Mia. She went over to her place and they discussed the situation over steaming hot tea and samosas.

Mia was glad that at last Ragini had found a normal suitor in the sense that his thinking was aligned with Ragini's and was not weird like the earlier ones. But the fact that he was not divorced was worrisome. Ragini felt anxious and confused. If she went ahead with Mani, there was no likelihood of an early marriage. There was even a chance that marriage might not happen if Mani and his wife made up. On the other hand, she had started to like Mani and didn't want to let him go. Maybe she was falling for him and she wanted to continue to fall.

The dilemma was proving to be unsettling for Ragini. After some thought Mia came up with a possible solution. Mani had been honest about his situation, he was not in the same city, he was not even pressing to meet her. So Ragini would do well to treat him purely as a friend for the time being. She could interact with him and find out more about him and his family. She should not see him as a probable husband but only as a friend, since she liked him. Once the status of his divorce got clear, Ragini could make a decision, provided she still wanted to go ahead. The divorce issue could be a blessing in disguise as it would force Ragini to evaluate everything instead of rushing into a marriage.

That made sense. Ragini nodded in agreement but still felt dejected. Why couldn't things be simple?

"Dear girl, it's all destiny," Mia tried to soothe her. "Remember the words of the Baba you took me to? He said 'You will definitely remarry',"

Mia mimicked the Baba and despite her troubles, Ragini smiled. She also spoke to Kamini, whose view was more or less the same as Mia's.

And so, Ragini found a friend in Mani. They started talking on a daily basis. Mani understood her discomfort about his marital status and tried to put her at ease by sharing details of his troubled first marriage.

Soon after getting admitted to MBA, Mani had fallen in love with the good looking but rather tempestuous classmate Varsha Arora. Varsha was a typical pampered, spoilt brat, being the only daughter of rich parents, who had a business in Pune. Mani cared for her deeply and felt protective towards her. Varsha, too, had gradually become drawn towards him and they soon became known as a committed couple in college. While both got good job offers after their MBA, Varsha was keen on marrying Mani but not so keen for a job. She would often tell Mani that she only wanted to be taken care of. And the smitten Mani would promise that. Varsha's parents were not so enthused as they felt Varsha could get a much better partner, someone who was of their level and status. Their reluctance made Mani's family apprehensive about the marriage. However, both of them were adamant. So they got married and that too with all the pomp and show, as Varsha desired.

Mani was posted in Mumbai and they enjoyed setting up their nest, as Mani called it. But soon the marriage ran into trouble because of the interference of Varsha's parents who wanted their only child to live a life of luxury. Varsha did not understand the financial problems Mani would have if she splurged without thought. Soon Mani's salary appeared insufficient and she started relying on her parents for her indulgences. This annoyed Mani and he asked her to take up a job instead. But she did not want to pursue a job and had started dreaming of joining her parents' business. They began having quarrels regularly. Mani was patient because he really cared for her and hoped that she would soon gain some sense. He tried his best to deal politely with her parents and keep them at a reasonable distance at the same time.

However, things became bad when Mani lost his job due to recession. As he struggled to find another job, instead of support, Varsha reacted with taunts and sarcasm and so the couple grew apart.

Varsha's parents, with a "we told you so" attitude started attacking Mani and even his family even more. One day, after a terrible fight, Varsha moved out and went to Pune to stay with her parents. Mani meanwhile got a job in Bangalore, but Varsha refused to join him. She told him how unhappy he made her and she did not want to live in Bangalore. Mani was dismayed. He had been trying for rapprochement for the past two years now. Varsha wanted him to come to Pune and look after her father's textile business. Mani was unwilling. His self-respect did not allow that. His professional aspirations were different. Besides,

Varsha didn't seem to want children or have anything to do with Mani's family.

Mani was growing frustrated with her demands and behaviour. He had started feeling that his one-sided efforts were not going to yield any results. Varsha was not showing any interest in being with him. Her parents were acting in a rude manner and had several times told him to stop harassing their daughter if he could not agree with her conditions. After trying for so long, Mani was feeling emotionally drained and willing to let go. There had been almost no communication between him and Varsha for several months.

Mani had realized that somewhere in all this battle, their love had flown out of the window and he wanted to move on. His family, which was genuinely worried for him, had also agreed last month for the divorce and that's when he had put up the profile on the website. Maybe, he confessed, he wanted to let Varsha know somehow that he was finally free of her, emotionally.

Ragini could easily identify with his pain. She liked his straightforwardness. She felt that Mani had given a long rope to Varsha and she had taken advantage of his feelings. Ragini felt drawn to Mani. He was the kind of person she wanted to spend the rest of her life with. She started confiding in him about her own fears of being alone. She shared with him her trials and tribulations of the past year. When she realized Mani was actually laughing at some of her encounters, she felt the absurdity of them, too, and their laughing together became her catharsis, wiping away all her sadness and allaying all her fears.

In one such conversation, Ragini brought up the question of marriage. "What if she doesn't give you divorce and we are not able to marry?" she asked.

"Well, I haven't proposed to you yet," Mani replied mischievously and Ragini blushed for being so bold. "But yes, seriously speaking, knowing how stubborn she can be and how she hates to be defeated, it is very likely that she won't give divorce easily. How about a live-in?"

Though Mani was clearly joking, Ragini found herself blushing again. She thought of her father and said a vehement no. But she knew she wouldn't mind waiting for Mani to get out of his situation, even if it took long.

One day, after nearly a month of talking every day and some romance, Mani said that he was coming to Delhi to discuss his divorce papers with his family lawyer before sending the notice to Varsha. And since Lucknow was not very far from Delhi, he was definitely going to visit her.

Ragini was ecstatic with the thought that she would meet Mani soon. She was also happy that this time she had not initiated any talk of a meeting. She immediately told Mia and Kamini, who shared her joy but at the same time warned her from going overboard. Ragini understood their concerns. But her delight at meeting Mani was stronger than any of these apprehensions.

Sessions at the beauty parlour followed. She changed her hairstyle again and got a stylish cut. Her pretty face glowed with happiness and she looked attractive, ready to meet her Prince Charming.

The day finally dawned when Mani was to come to Lucknow. He had reached Delhi a couple of days earlier and finalized the draft of the divorce notice with his lawyer. He had tried to contact Varsha through a common friend to see if she would agree for a divorce with mutual consent, but it had been futile. Hence, he would send the notice and then come to Lucknow.

They had agreed to meet in the evening at a popular restaurant for dinner. The morning dragged on and Ragini found herself feeling restless at work. As she moved around listlessly, there was a call from the reception that she had a visitor. When she went over to see who it was, she couldn't believe her eyes. It was Mani!

"I couldn't wait till evening," he said sheepishly and they both just stood and grinned at each other, suddenly at a loss for words.

Ragini composed herself, took him to her cabin and offered him a seat and some tea. She told herself he was pleasant looking and he had an air of shyness around him which was quite appealing. If she had known Mani's thoughts at that moment, she would have been surprised to know that he was also thinking the same about her.

"So here we are," said Mani as he sipped the tea. "I thought I would catch you unawares."

"Yes, you certainly did. How did it go with the lawyer and the notice?" Ragini asked.

"It was fine. As the first step, as advised by the lawyer, I've sent her a simple notice stating all the facts of our separation and asking for divorce. Now she has to reply and the family court will then fix a date for the hearing. I'm not sure what she will say in her reply."

"Yes, that's the standard procedure," replied Ragini. She should know, she thought – she had already been through it herself.

"It is going to be a long haul. Since I am filing for divorce from Delhi, which is my permanent residence and also the place of our wedding, I will be coming to Delhi for the hearings and that means we can meet rather often. That is the silver lining," Mani said in one breath, looking tenderly at Ragini.

Though both Mani's statement and expression pleased her, she could sense that the divorce situation was not very bright and that affected her happy mood. However, she reminded herself of her resolve to find happiness with Mani as a friend and a companion and brought her thoughts back to the present. They chatted less and stayed silent more, continuing to take in each other. The mutual attraction was definitely building up.

Ragini asked Mani to stay for lunch but he said no. They had to meet for dinner, anyway. While leaving, he tried to give her a hug, but Ragini drew back, thinking of her past episodes. If it surprised Mani, he didn't show it. Ragini resolved to be clear in her mind as to how far she was ready to go with him.

In the evening she dressed in a formal suit, thinking it would befit the candlelight dinner they were having.

Mani was staying with a college friend and had borrowed his car for the evening. Looking smart in a blue check shirt and jeans, he picked her up from her house. Ragini had assumed they would go to the place already decided but she found Mani in a completely different mood.

"Let's drive around for a while," he said, "I want to see the city." And with that he zipped around as Ragini guided him.

Ragini understood now what he had written in his profile as Mani drove so fast around the city. She recollected the silence between them just hours earlier when they had first met. She felt a tinge of warm glow inside her and felt happy that things were turning out right for them. She enjoyed the drive more than she had thought she would. She kept explaining the city's high points to Mani who had not visited Lucknow earlier. In her excited state, even the regular sights looked so different now.

Mani drove towards the Delhi highway and asked Ragini if she was hungry. When Ragini shyly nodded a yes, Mani stopped in front of a road side eatery and gallantly held the car door open for her.

Ragini stepped out, laughing inwardly at having dressed up for a formal dinner. Her dreams of a candlelight dinner were gone, but she liked the thought of a moonlit one even more.

As they had their rustic but delicious food, the tender moonlight enveloped them and Ragini felt soaked in the sheer rays of love. She decided she wanted to go the whole way with Mani and desperately fought the small inner voice telling her to hold back. "He isn't even divorced yet," said the voice.

"You appear lost," Mani gently broke through her thoughts. And before she could say anything, he continued, "I know what are you thinking. You wanted a conventional romantic evening and you are wondering what are we doing here, in the middle of nowhere, in a dhaba with desi food. But my dear, this is how I view life – spontaneously. One should be able to let go of any dogma and just live. What do you think?"

Ragini remembered Mani's profile on the matrimonial site and was touched by his transparency. She nodded her head in agreement. She was in a daze, feeling too much in love to make rational comments. She wanted to be in his arms but Mani appeared to show no such desire. He was happy to just be with her and enjoy her company.

Wanting to get to a place where they could get cosy, she asked if they could leave once the dinner was over. Mani thought she wanted to go back home and called for the bill quickly. They headed back, driving slowly and enjoying the soft music coming on the radio.

When they reached her home, before Ragini could invite him in, Mani bid her goodnight with a chaste peck on the cheek and left.

Back home, Ragini relived the evening. It had been much more pleasant than what she had anticipated. She had been drawn towards Mani and had wanted to go further but Mani had shown no inclination towards getting physical. This was the only thing that puzzled her. Maybe it was because she had turned him away in office, she consoled herself, and now he was being the perfect gentleman. She tried to sleep and when she couldn't, she dialled Mia.

Mia heard about her date and the anti-climax at the end. She gave an exasperated laugh. "Ragini, when will you find that one, perfect Raymond man? When the man makes advances there is a problem, when he doesn't, there is still a problem. What do you want?"

"You know what I mean," Ragini replied. "When we have connected so well, Mani could have ..."

Mia comforted her by explaining that it was absolutely correct on Mani's part to hold on for a while. After all, it was only their first date. Tomorrow they had one more day together. If Ragini was so keen, she could well make some clear moves. With this final advice, Mia disconnected and Ragini fell asleep, thinking of what she would wear the next day.

She woke up next morning to find a message on her phone from Mani.

> Sweetheart, it was a lovely evening. I'm still under the spell. Hope the magic will last forever.

Ragini felt she was in heaven. In a state of bliss, she did some preparations for the evening dinner. The plan was to watch a movie with Mani in the evening and then have dinner together at home.

The movie *Garam Masala* was a breezy comedy. As the picture started, Ragini and Mani held hands like young lovers and Mani kept giving reassuring squeezes. After the movie, they went to her home for dinner as they had planned.

Over dinner Ragini talked of her job and how she envisioned her future. While Mani appreciated her neatly kept home and the delicious dinner, Ragini felt him to be a bit more quiet than usual. While Ragini could feel anticipation building up inside her, Mani again showed no signs of wanting to even hold hands, leave alone anything more.

After dinner, Ragini put on some ghazals and discovered that there was no common ground there. Mani was fond of rock and pop and she barely listened to that. She invited Mani to search the small storeroom for some pop CDs left by Mia, which Mani promptly got up to do.

With Jagjit Singh's soulful voice in the background, Ragini mustered up her courage, followed Mani to the storeroom and called him from behind. With a start, Mani turned around and they found themselves in each other's arms. Ragini turned her face upwards to kiss Mani and so they lip-locked in the small space, music and everything else forgotten.

Ragini found herself kissing Mani with a passion she did not know existed in her. Mani responded with equal fervour and almost carried her to the bedroom. Mani's touch was electrifying and passion reigned as time stood still. Their lovemaking was ferocious and only afterwards, as they lay spent, did Ragini realize what had happened. However, she was feeling too satiated to do any analysis. She snuggled into Mani, who was caressing her tenderly.

Mani was also totally immersed in the moment and didn't want to leave. His flight back was in the morning, so they decided to go and get his luggage from his friend's house. Mani drove the borrowed car. Ragini was silent throughout the drive. After initial attempts to talk, Mani's earlier quietness returned, too. Mani introduced her to his friend, who didn't prod them much. They took a cab back and completed the return journey in the same mood and reached Ragini's home in silence.

"Look, perhaps you are feeling we should not have gone ahead but it's okay," said Mani as he held her hand and tried to lighten up Ragini's mood. "Shall I call Mia here if that will help?"

Ragini was amused. She was not an innocent young girl anymore. The lovemaking had happened on her initiation and here was poor Mani trying to console her! In reply, she moved closer to Mani, gave him a hug and rested her head on his chest.

As Mani kept stroking her hair, the cosy warmth between them soon replaced the awkwardness that had crept in. Ragini regained her poise and coaxed by Mani started speaking out her doubts to him. Their marriage wasn't certain yet, they lived in different cities, their families might not agree to their marriage, how were things to work out? How could they retain and build this relationship? She spoke emotionally, from her heart.

"Are you certain you want to be with me?" asked Mani. "I for sure don't want to lose this precious relationship. Marriage may not be soon, but worse comes to worse, will you be prepared to live with me without a formal marriage?" he asked, holding her tenderly.

Ragini again was touched by the honesty in his words and whispered yes for everything that he had said. Relaxing, Mani put on the TV and surfed through the channels. An old movie came on.

"So then, where do you keep the items required for prayers?" he asked.

Perplexed, Ragini pointed towards her small temple near the bedroom, which she kept covered. Mani went to it and returned holding something in his hands.

"Come here," he said. As Ragini moved forward, he opened the small box of kumkum powder he was holding and showed it to Ragini. Ragini looked at him quizzically and Mani then pointed towards the TV screen. Ragini saw the title of the movie – *Maang Bharo Sajna* – and though

Mani's intent was serious, she couldn't help laughing. With laughter sealing the moment, they both went to bed. They made love again, this time slowly, both of them savouring the pleasure before they went to sleep.

The next morning was bright and sunny and though Mani was leaving, Ragini managed to retain a positive frame of mind.

Mani left with promises and hugs. Ragini was left feeling alone but happy at the sudden turn of events in her life. She called up Kamini and had a long conversation with her about her feelings for Mani. She obviously hid the lovemaking part from Kamini – Mia would understand these things but Kamini would only get troubled.

Kamini was not happy with the situation because the fact remained that Mani was not legally free to marry her and it was totally uncertain when his divorce would come through. She, as always, cautioned her. She reminded her of the harsh reality in front of her and told her to not get totally drowned in her emotions. Ragini realized the sense in her sane words but was too much in love to act upon them.

"Didi, we have decided to take each day as it comes. Divorce or no divorce, no one can take away our companionship and that's what matters. At least I'm no longer alone," said Ragini.

During the day, she often caught herself humming. Mani called to say he had reached Bangalore safely and Ragini felt complete as she talked to him.

In the evening Mia cooked dinner for her and listened eagerly to all the developments.

"What are you saying!" she exclaimed as Ragini shyly told her the details. Mia could not believe that Ragini had dropped all her barriers with Mani, even though they had talked about it earlier. The Goa trip had certainly made her lose her inhibitions, she thought. Her wonderment turned to delight as she saw how contented her friend was feeling.

"You are on the right track, things will resolve themselves," was her final verdict as both friends hugged each other in happiness.

Days passed for Ragini in kaleidoscopic hues of bliss, anxiety, love and daydreams. There was no development in the divorce case as Varsha did not reply to the notice but there was progress by leaps and bounds in her relationship with Mani.

He surprised her by visiting her once more over a weekend and again the days and the nights turned magical. Mani had brought a bright Bangalore silk sari for her and Ragini looked resplendent as she draped it and paraded in front of him. They went shopping and had fun eating the famous Hazrat Ganj food.

Mani met Mia and hit off well with her. Mia was assessing Mani initially but when she saw the strong chemistry between her friend and him, she also relaxed. Ragini even got Kamini to speak to Mani on the phone, but she didn't let out that Mani was staying in her house. Kamini understood her sister's joy but wondered how it would work out.

Ragini was unbelievably happy in Mani's company and as they made love tenderly, she felt all her doubts and fears slipping away. Mani was also totally relaxed and involved with her. Their easy camaraderie had strengthened into a strong lovers' bond. By the time Mani left on Sunday, Ragini was convinced that this was the true love she had been seeking all this time. She and Mani may not be able to marry but at least they were building up a comfortable relationship.

They talked of future, too. Mani told her he was going to try to take a transfer to Delhi, where his company's head office was and Ragini said she would also do that.

"We will have to meet each other's families," said Mani. He had told her that he wanted his family to accept her and have a good equation with her. He often talked fondly about them and Ragini felt she knew them all already. She knew that his father was strict but affectionate and that his mother was a simple and religious lady. His younger sister Kavya had recently got married in Mumbai. His elder brother Dinesh and his wife Archana had a five-year-old son, Kartik. Ragini could already visualize Shrey bonding well with Kartik. She marvelled at the fact that both of them loved their families so much and their family's approval mattered so much to both of them. Mani particularly wanted to meet Kamini as he knew how close the two sisters were. He jokingly asked her if he would win Kamini's approval.

Ragini was also thinking along the same lines. She wanted to get the families involved so that they were aware of the developments. Mia also told her to nurture the bonds with Mani's family as things were likely to remain the same on the divorce front, at least for a while.

It needed the hand of God to change the situation completely and most unexpectedly.

In the early hours of a chilly December morning, a phone call woke up Ragini. Still half-awake, she heard Mani's voice at the other end. What Mani said jolted her into complete wakefulness.

"Varsha is no more," he said. He sounded shaken and distraught.

"What are you saying? There must be some mistake. Are you sure?" She was too shocked to say anything coherent.

Mani said a common friend had called him from Pune giving details of Varsha's death due to liver failure, owing to a rare and fatal form of hepatitis. She had developed acute jaundice which had worsened, leading to severe complications. Her family had been planning to shift her to Delhi for a major surgery but before that could happen, she had developed multi-organ failure and had gone into a coma for nearly a week before passing away.

Mani could not speak much and Ragini too was very shocked at the sad news. During the day, though she went to office, her thoughts remained with Mani as she pondered over the unpredictability of life and relationships. A moment was enough to sniff out a life. She kept thinking of Varsha and the short, unfulfilled life she had led. She thought of Mani and the trauma he was undergoing.

It was much later that a tiny voice from inside her said she and Mani could marry now. However, Ragini could not feel the joy that she would have otherwise felt at this thought. She met Mia in the evening and both friends discussed the sudden turn of events. Mia tried to cheer her up but Ragini remained distressed. She called up Kamini who also could not believe the news of demise of Varsha. Kamini told her to be supportive of Mani at this hour.

"He needs you and you must put him first as of now. All the rest will fall in place," advised Kamini wisely.

*****

Second Chance

Mani continued to remain distraught. He tried to contact Varsha's parents but they turned him away. They curtly told him that they did not want anything to do with him. This saddened him further. Most conversations Ragini had with Mani were about Varsha, and he talked of both the good and bad experiences with her. Ragini thought it was natural and kept herself composed.

Mani's family had also been shocked by the passing away of Varsha and he decided to come to Delhi to meet them. Ragini was keen to meet him and so when Mani asked her, she readily agreed to come to Delhi for a day. She took a morning flight to Delhi, which got delayed due to fog. They met briefly for lunch in a restaurant in Connaught Place. The weather was gloomy and did nothing to lift their spirits. Mani was in a sombre mood and Ragini was also silent. They held hands as they ordered food and ate quietly.

While coming to Delhi, Ragini had thought that perhaps Mani would introduce her to his parents. But on meeting him she realized that the shock of Varsha's demise had been so much that Mani was in no mood to talk of marriage. She could clearly see that he was not his usual self. She would have to hold back.

However, she had a pleasant surprise when Mani introduced her to his elder brother Dinesh and his wife Archana when they came to the restaurant to pick him up. She didn't know that Mani had told them everything about their relationship and she made a mental note to quiz Mani about it.

They were a pleasant couple, obviously concerned for Mani. Ragini could feel Archana scrutinizing her, but she calmly remained her usual self and soon Archana became friendly. They dropped Ragini at the airport for her flight back to Lucknow. Archana and Ragini exchanged phone numbers. Though marriage was on everyone's mind, no one raised the topic, looking at Mani's state. Mani stayed back in Delhi for a few days. On reaching Lucknow, Ragini had a feeling that the trip was somewhat of an anti-climax. However, she soon put that feeling away.

She thought of her brief meeting with Dinesh and Archana and wondered about meeting the rest of Mani's family.

Ragini's family, meanwhile, paid her a surprise visit. She told Kamini and Aman again that Mani was the one for her and things should progress towards marriage soon. Kamini and Aman were delighted. As she hugged Ragini, there were tears in Kamini's eyes as she remembered the fateful day of her divorce and then her entire journey of trying to marry again. Kamini couldn't wait to meet Mani and his family.

Their father did not speak much, but the way he put his hand on Ragini's head, both sisters understood his blessings were there with her. Aman grilled her a bit on Mani's career and appeared satisfied with his qualifications and profile. Even Shrey appeared excited. Kamini and Aman asked Ragini about the next steps and Ragini told them she was waiting to hear from Mani.

After her family left, Ragini resumed her routine and waited for Mani to get back. She felt both elated and uncertain – elated because her quest was getting over and uncertain because there was no finality yet about the date of the wedding.

After the Delhi visit and as the year drew to an end, Mani seemed to change. He became more taciturn. Their conversations reduced. Ragini kept asking him what was wrong but to no avail. Mani gradually withdrew from the relationship and went into a shell.

Mani had thought he would recover once the initial shock was over, but he found the opposite happening. He was consumed by thoughts of Varsha. He thought of how they had met and how pleasantly crazy Varsha had been. He remembered their marriage and their dreams of a rosy future. He recalled the road trip to Lonavala and how Varsha had dared him to make love to her right there in the car, by the side of the highway. He had readily agreed. He thought of how the fights had gradually increased and the relationship had turned sour. He also remembered the innumerable times when her parents had been downright rude to him.

After office, as he spent one lonely evening after another, he started feeling guilty and felt he himself was responsible for the failure of his marriage. He should have been able to handle Varsha and sort out the mess. And then a bigger fear started to engulf him. What if he failed Ragini too? She was such a sweet girl who loved him wholeheartedly, but will he be a good husband? What if he hurt Ragini and she also left him? Perhaps he was destined to live alone and there was no point in chasing what was not in his destiny.

He was hesitant to share these thoughts with Ragini. What could she possibly say? He thought distancing himself from Ragini was the only way out. He knew in the bottom of his heart that this was not the right way to resolve the issues. He had committed to Ragini and she trusted him. Yet his demons became so strong that rational thinking eluded him. He went about his life like a zombie. He stopped taking Ragini's calls. He just did not want to do anything and wanted to be alone, by himself.

Ragini kept the phone down. After her fifth call of the day to Mani went unanswered, she was almost beside herself with anxiety. She went over to Mia and told her what was happening. "Mani could not do this to me," Ragini kept saying. Mia was also worried but she tried not to show it and attempted to soothe Ragini.

"See, there must be some explanation. He was all right when you met him in Delhi few days ago.

He even introduced you to his brother and sister-in-law." Mia spoke as if she was reassuring herself.

Ragini was puzzled. She went through every moment of her Delhi visit but could not figure out what had gone wrong. Mia asked her about her last conversation with Mani. Ragini remembered the terse conversation almost a week ago. Mani had been sounding forlorn and Ragini had asked him what was wrong.

"Nothing and everything," Mani had replied cryptically.

Then, after a brief conversation, he had kept the phone down abruptly. Since then, he had not answered her calls nor replied to her texts, other than a short message that he wanted to be alone.

Ragini was not merely annoyed but greatly disturbed too. Mia was also in a quandary. On one hand she did not want Ragini to get scared unnecessarily, but on the other, Mani's behaviour was worrisome.

"I think, he only wants to come to terms with what has happened. After all, Varsha's death was a shock and maybe it is hitting him now," she tried to console Ragini.

"But this silence is not acceptable," Ragini said agitatedly. "He could have shared what he is feeling with me. Why avoid me at this juncture? He can't simply decide unilaterally to cut-off like this. I feel like going to Bangalore and shaking him up."

"No, you will look desperate," Mia advised. If her calls were not welcome, God only knew how he would react if she went there. Maybe he only wanted time alone and would soon get out of this. But even then, he could have talked it out with Ragini, thought Mia as she stirred the tea she was making.

"We have to think of some other way," she said, handing over a cup to Ragini.

Ragini was too angry and confused to think straight. Her thoughts went back to her recent past and she wondered if this would be yet another failed attempt. Her remarriage was not going to happen.

"Hey, why don't you talk to Archana? You have her number, don't you?" Mia asked Ragini.

"But won't it look odd to involve her? First, I should be clear that Mani wants me in his life," Ragini said with a sad look on her face.

"We must not jump to conclusions. It is also a matter of worry that Mani is not responding. It's been a week since you spoke to him. So convey your concern to Archana. After all, you are going to marry into that family. Start building your relationships now," Mia again advised her.

Ragini mumbled a bit about her fate but realized that she had only two options. She could either go to Bangalore and in all likelihood make a fool of herself or follow Mia's advice and see what happened.

She did not do anything for a couple of days. On the third day, when she again saw herself trapped in an aeroplane in her dream, she knew she had to act. It was New Year's Eve and the turbulent year was finally coming to an end. She thought of all that had happened in the last few months, remembered her anguish when she had been deceived and her happiness when she had found Mani. She had certainly not imagined that the year would end on this uncertain note. She decided to call up Archana.

"Hello," Archana greeted her warmly. "How are you?"

Ragini tried to respond normally by wishing her a happy new year but Archana sensed her despondency.

"What happened, is everything all right?" she asked with concern.

"No, nothing is all right," Ragini said emotionally. "Mani has withdrawn and is avoiding me completely. He hasn't talked to me for more than a week. I'm worried also. His last message was that I should leave him alone. I don't know what is wrong with him," Ragini almost sobbed.

"Was there a fight or something?" asked Archana.

"No, none. After the time when we met in Delhi, Mani avoided talking to me and seems to have gone into a shell.

"Is he talking regularly to all of you?"

"Well, he calls Dinesh regularly but of late

Dinesh has been busy in work. I will ask Dinesh to have a word with him. You don't worry and try to relax," reassured Archana.

Ragini felt some relief in her tense state. She again dialled Mani but his phone was switched off. She sent him a message wishing him a happy new year and asked him to call her back.

She wanted to spend the evening alone but Mia would not let that happen. She landed at her home with a bottle of red wine and both friends laughed as they remembered Goa and Neil Ribeiro.

The first morning of the New Year was like any other and yet it was different. The chirping of birds sounded merrier, the wind was breezier and even the fog felt welcoming. Ragini woke up and remembered the pleasant evening with Mia. She looked at her phone expectantly but there was no message from Mani. She called up Kamini and wished everybody in Banaras. Kamini could make out from Ragini's voice that there was no change in the situation with Mani and refrained from asking anything. Instead, she asked Ragini to dress up and welcome the New Year with a positive mind. She also asked Ragini to visit her soon.

It was a Sunday. Ragini dressed in a new turquoise sari and went to the nearby market. All around, everybody was in a celebratory frame of mind. Her mood lifted a bit and she dialled Mani again, but to no avail. Sighing, she went about her daily chores and busied herself in sprucing up her apartment.

She spent the evening alone as Mia was out with her office friends for a party. Kamini was also out with Aman and Shrey. She put on some ghazals and cooked herself a rice dish with onions and potatoes. She sent new year messages to some of her colleagues and then suddenly, tired of being alone, she sat with her laptop and logged into DivorceeMatrimony.com. She had not visited the site for a considerable period of time.

She saw her profile with a wry smile and was surprised to see a message from Ravish Mitra, her earlier failed attempt at marriage. Curious, she opened it and read.

> Ragini, I want to apologize for my behaviour. Boorish, wasn't I? Please forgive me. I've done a lot of thinking in these days and I realized that I was showing very extreme behaviour, in fact chauvinistic. You were very patient and rational with me but I was thinking of only taking from a relationship. I was so scarred by the experience of my first marriage that I could not think straight. And so now I want to simply say sorry. I could have called you but I didn't have the courage. Your response will indicate if we can still move further.
> Regards,
> Ravish.
>
> P.S. Rajma is also welcome now ;-)

Ragini was perplexed. She recalled her conversations with Ravish and how unreasonable he had been. And now he seemed to have had a change of heart. She didn't know how to react and whether even to respond to him. She decided to sleep over it and see how she felt in the morning.

Thankfully, she slept peacefully and woke up fresh. It was a working day and she had to get ready for office. After a light breakfast of porridge and fruit, she first called up Mani. This time the call went through but there was no response. She then read Ravish's message again. Still confused, she called up Mia and asked her to meet in evening.

After an uneventful day in office, she met Mia. They decided to go out for dinner and settled for Pizza Choice.

Mia was noncommittal as she heard Ragini speak about Ravish and his apology. She picked up a slice of pizza and said, "What do you want to do? You have moved on and this apology should be of no relevance. Don't tell me that you are having some other thoughts?"

Ragini played around with her pizza, deep in thoughts. She felt badly hurt by Mani's behaviour and had reached a point where she wanted to stop thinking about him. Maybe engaging with Ravish would take her mind off Mani.

"What's the harm?" She finally spoke aloud. "You keep saying have fun and now instead of this marriage business, where everybody is taking me for a ride, why shouldn't I really have fun and forget about sincerity for a while at least?"

Her strong response amazed Mia and she knew she had to stop Ragini from being reckless. "You let this fellow Ravish be. A leopard cannot change his spots. Why, he didn't even want you to work. And now suddenly, just because he says he is sorry, you want to give him a chance? I would rather you go to Bangalore and sort out things with Mani first," Mia said forcefully.

But something had got into Ragini. Months of swinging between hope and despair had taken a toll on her ability to think rationally. After dinner, she bade good bye to Mia and came home, only to start organizing her cupboard. Her mind kept going back to Mani and their happy moments and their lovemaking. She could not understand why he was behaving in such a manner. She thought he would ask her to marry him and he was doing everything but that.

Tormented by her thoughts, she left the pile of clothes and called up Kamini. Kamini understood her state of mind and was worried for her.

"Just take it easy. If you want, I will try and speak to Mani," she said.

But Ragini was in no mood for any such move. She wanted Mani to realize for himself what he was doing was wrong.

She then sent a simple reply to Ravish saying it was good to hear from him and perhaps they could talk.

*****

Second Chance 2

Dinesh knocked at the door of Mani's apartment at 100-Feet Road in Bangalore, glad to be away from the foggy, January cold of Delhi but worried about his younger brother. Archana had told him about Ragini's call. He had called up Mani and asked him what was going on. Mani had not talked much but murmured that he wanted to be left alone and could not take the chance of hurting Ragini in any way. Dinesh understood him and realized that something would have to be done to bring Mani out of this state. So here he was in Bangalore, hoping to knock some sense into his younger brother.

If Mani was surprised to see Dinesh, he didn't show it. He gave a weak smile as he welcomed him. The apartment was small and neatly kept. Dinesh was relieved – he had been expecting a mess. He had rarely visited Mani earlier because of Varsha's attitude and now he wished he had stepped in at that time too. Dragging his mind to the present, sipping coffee, he relished the dosa–sambhar Mani had ordered and then without much preamble, came straight to the point.

"What are you up to? Why have you withdrawn from Ragini? In fact, from all of us? Your calls have reduced and you don't seem your normal self. What is wrong?"

"I don't know what is wrong," Mani replied quietly. "Varsha's demise has impacted me far more than I thought it would."

"But you were already living separately for a while and there was no love lost between you," Dinesh replied.

"I know, it's not that. It's more of a feeling that probably I failed her and I am somewhat responsible for what ultimately happened to her. I could not take care of her properly. And the way her parents have been shunning me, it makes me feel that something must be wrong with me," said Mani and became silent for a while.

Dinesh coaxed him to speak whatever was there in his heart and Mani almost broke down trying to do that.

"Why did she have to die? She didn't give me a chance. We did love each other and could have made it work. And now she's gone forever, leaving so many unspoken thoughts and words. She was dying and I was sending her a divorce notice. Can you imagine what she must have thought?"

After a while he continued, "As it is, she had started despising me because I didn't earn enough. On top of that, I must have appeared so cruel and insensitive. I wish I could have at least spoken to her one last time. I wish she had not gone in such a manner."

Dinesh let him speak. He realized that all the pent-up emotions needed to be released. It was important to let them out so that they could dissipate.

"And now I'm left with this gnawing doubt that I'm not good enough," continued Mani. "If I was not good enough for Varsha, what is the guarantee that I will be good enough for Ragini? I can't hurt Ragini. She has already undergone so much in her first marriage as well as later in her search for a second marriage. She deserves a simple, uncomplicated, loving life. And look at me, I'm a wreck now. I keep thinking of Varsha, keep thinking where I went wrong. She is there even in my dreams and at times and I wake up in a cold sweat," Mani said.

Dinesh heard him patiently. He had anticipated some catharsis and was glad that Mani had opened up. It could only get better from here. He handed him a glass of water and asked pointedly, "What is Ragini's fault in all this?"

Mani was silent. He did not want to talk further. But Dinesh persisted.

"Of course, Ragini is not to blame for any of this," Mani finally acknowledged.

"Then, why are you making her suffer by your sudden withdrawal? You owe her an explanation. You made a commitment to her and you wanted to marry her. You even made her meet Archana and me. Now you can't go silent completely. The poor girl is only trying to reach out to you and you are not responding. It's not right," Dinesh said, rather sternly.

"I felt it was the proper course of action to distance myself from her to ensure that she did not get hurt."

"You know she is feeling hurt even now. You wanted a life partner, you put out a profile and when you found someone, you are turning your back because of self-doubt. You wanted a second chance and now you are throwing it away. Today you are regretting about Varsha, tomorrow it may well be about Ragini. Don't live a life full of regrets. Have faith in yourself and in your emotions. And even if you have any doubts, talk to Ragini about them. You are belittling her and your relationship by staying away. She is a sensible girl. You know her better than I do. You must trust her to do the right thing. But do it before it's too late," Dinesh concluded.

Dinesh spent the day with Mani, insisting on taking him out and they went strolling down the iconic Brigade Road and had dinner there. Though Dinesh did not bring up the subject of Ragini again, it remained a palpable thought between them. Dinesh sensed that Mani was doing some introspection. Before he left, he again advised Mani to count his blessings and come out of his self-induced isolation.

Mani was in a daze after Dinesh's visit. The churning of emotions left him drained. However, he found himself less tormented by Varsha's thoughts. He looked at his phone and saw the numerous calls and messages by Ragini. He felt guilty as he realized the anguish he must have caused Ragini. He had to right the wrong he had done. As the dark clouds of his sombre thoughts lifted, he felt lighter and somewhat his usual self again. Earlier, while his heart had told him to turn to Ragini for solace, his mind had said he had to go through this alone, in order to find a final solution. Dinesh's visit had acted as a facilitator. And now, purged of the burden he was carrying, his rational self told him to shut the door on the past and look towards a warm future with Ragini. However, now that he had created a gap between her and himself, he felt unsure about how to bridge it.

*****

Ragini found Ravish waiting for her in the lobby as she entered the Clarks Awadh hotel. Ravish had eagerly responded to her email and had called her immediately. He had profusely apologized again and told her clearly that he wanted to be with her and marry her.

Ragini was not sure. She was still smarting from the way Mani had behaved. Her heart refused to believe that it could end in such a fashion and yet the total silence from Mani was bringing out a strong reaction in her. She had agreed to meet Ravish, though both Mia and Kamini were not in favour. Ravish had lost no time in coming to Lucknow and now here she was, walking with trepidation towards him.

Ravish was a fair, good-looking man and had an amiable manner, in contrast to how stiff he had earlier sounded on phone. Ragini relaxed a bit as she shook hands with him and he led her towards the restaurant. Knowing his fondness for food, Ragini let him order and leaned back in a comfortable manner. Thoughts of Mani started to form in her mind but she firmly pushed them away and started to talk to Ravish animatedly, asking about his daughter.

"I cannot tell you how delighted I am that you could forgive me and agree to meet me. Trust me, I realize I was rude to you. I was reeling under the effects of my ex-wife's actions and somehow my reactions got targeted at you. I'm extremely sorry," Ravish said, looking deep into her eyes and holding her hand.

Ragini felt a trifle uncomfortable with the increasing intimacy he was expressing and tried to steer the conversation to a safer track. She asked him about his sudden change of heart and if his strong desire to have a non-working wife had also changed. Ravish explained how his daughter had started yearning for a mother figure and he had intensified his search for a life partner. However, he had been unable to get Ragini out of his mind and had decided to accept her terms for remarriage.

"So now you decide whatever you choose. Whether you work, you cook non-vegetarian food or anything for that matter, it is all up to you. I'm seriously head-over-heels in love with you and really want your yes as an answer."

Ragini was surprised at his intensity and toyed around with the delicious biryani thinking of a suitable answer. Her mind was in turmoil. Her moments together with Mani appeared in front of her. She focused her thoughts towards Ravish and tried to enjoy his company. But it was an effort and not very successful.

"Well, at least enjoy the dessert, if not my company," Ravish said candidly and Ragini blushed guiltily. She really had no answer for Ravish and she decided to be honest with him.

"Ravish, look, it's very nice that you realized that you were being unreasonable. But all this is rather sudden for me and I want some time before I give you my answer."

"Oh, I see," Ravish looked a bit disappointed and let down. "But I suppose, it's only fair. Yes, take time – but don't take too long. Till then let's continue to be in touch," he said almost beseechingly.

Ragini felt awkward. Things had moved far too quickly for her to make a rational decision. She told Ravish this and said she would like to leave. As Ravish settled the bill, he begged Ragini to do him a favour and come up to his room.

"I have got something for you and please don't say no. My daughter helped me select it and she would want to know if you liked it," Ravish requested. Ragini got swayed at the mention of his daughter and agreed, not realizing that she was breaking the cardinal rule of such meetings – never be alone with the date in a room or an isolated place.

As they came out of the lift and walked towards his room, Ravish held her hand and again Ragini felt uneasy. Thankfully the room was close by. As soon as they entered, Ragini saw the most exquisite Baluchari sari in white and red, on the bed. It was a piece of art and Ragini felt touched, her discomfort leaving her for a moment. But before she could express her thanks, Ravish had grabbed her from behind and was trying to kiss her. He turned her around and his hands were everywhere, all over her, all the time saying, "Say yes, say yes."

Somehow Ragini managed to push him away, ran out of the room and quickly got into the lift. She was in panic. She caught a cab and was almost in tears by the time she reached home and flung herself on her bed. She had never imagined Ravish would try to force himself on her.

She called Mia, who immediately came over and hugged and consoled her. Mia wanted to lodge a complaint with the police but as Ragini calmed down, she thought better of it and decided instead to complain to the matrimony site. But more than that, Ragini wanted at that moment to be in Mani's arms. She realized how deeply she loved him and there could be no one else for her. The thought of his behaviour, coupled with what she had undergone made her break down, and she cried her heart out in Mia's arms before finally dozing off to sleep.

Looking at her state, Mia stayed the night with her and tried to cheer her up in the morning.

"Rise and shine dear," she said, handing her favourite masala tea to her and settling on her bed. She had a sleepless night, thinking about how vulnerable Ragini had been and vowing never to let her be in such a situation again. To divert her mind, she steered the conversation towards Ragini's upcoming birthday.

"What birthday?" Ragini dismissed the idea and was not inclined to plan for anything. Almost a year of trying to get married is no cause for celebration was her refrain. But Mia knew she was actually missing Mani and wished she could somehow get them to meet.

*****

Happy Birthday

As Mani realized that his future lay with Ragini and how unfair he had been to her, he wanted to make amends. He observed how her calls and messages had dwindled over the past few days and could visualize the angry state Ragini would be in. Sending only a message or calling up seemed too small an action. He knew he had to do something else to win Ragini back. His faith in Ragini's love was so strong that it didn't occur to him even for a moment that Ragini might spurn him. As he thought about what he could do, he recalled that Ragini's birthday was around the corner. It would be a perfect opportunity to meet and clear the air between them. Hurriedly, he started to make his travel plans.

*****

Though Ragini had brushed off Mia's idea to celebrate her birthday, Mia wanted to make it a memorable day for her. Both had refrained from telling Kamini about the details of Ragini's encounter with Ravish and had merely told her that he didn't seem suitable. Kamini wanted Ragini to cheer up and urged Mia to come to Banaras with Ragini to celebrate Ragini's birthday. But 30th January was Monday, a working day and it was difficult to get leave from office. Kamini asked them to come over on the weekend before the birthday instead, and Mia decided to do that as a surprise for Ragini. She told Ragini to pack her bags and be ready on Saturday morning and Ragini agreed reluctantly. Only when they sat in the cab, did Mia share the destination with her.

Mia's enthusiasm rubbed on to Ragini and she found herself in a cheerful mood as the journey progressed. Kamini was waiting for them with a sumptuous meal and hugged them warmly as they arrived. Ragini's father, Shrey and Aman were delighted too and it was a merry family that enjoyed the hot and delicious chola bhaturas and paav bhaji, followed by kesari kheer. If Ragini was thinking of Mani, she didn't show it and changed the topic when Kamini tried to broach it.

They had a leisurely evening, where the three girls laughed and talked as they made dinner together. The next day they decided to go for an early morning visit to the Kashi Vishwanath temple and seek blessings. The walk in the narrow lane up to the majestic temple reminded Ragini and Kamini of the many times they had accompanied their mother. Both sisters felt nostalgic as they had the view of the deity. Mia was also in a thoughtful mood and the three came back home, awed by the divine ambience. After a quick and simple lunch, Ragini and Mia started their journey back home, dozing off on the way.

On her birthday, Ragini blow-dried her tresses and dressed up in a new lavender silk sari. Her mind kept going back to Mani. Could he be so heartless as to not even wish her today? Her anticipation that he might call made her have a restless day at office and she could only absent-mindedly accept the greetings from her boss and colleagues.

In the evening, she changed into a pink suit, smiling at the thought of having worn both her favourite colours on the same day. She again checked her phone and sighed at seeing the empty screen before stepping out with Mia for their favourite pastime of watching a movie. The new release *Rang De Basanti* had rave reviews and both watched the well-made movie with admiration. After dinner at a restaurant in Hazrat Ganj, Mia got her to cut her a delicious butterscotch cake and wished her heartily. Mia's birthday present was a beautiful chikankari sari in baby pink colour and as both friends hugged, Mia sent a silent prayer up for her friend to find happiness. She had also stayed away from bringing up the subject of Mani but now she was determined to call him and ask for an explanation as she could not believe that he would not wish Ragini on her birthday. With that thought, she wished Ragini good night and went home.

Ragini also tried to settle for the night, her heart a trifle heavy with Mani's act of disappearance. She thought about the past months, her intimacy with Mani and then the sudden turn of events and felt sad again. However, determined not to let her birthday end on a sad note, she called up Kamini and chatted warmly with her about the day. Hanging up, she picked up 'Twilight', the new novel by Stephenie Meyer and, lost in the enticing world of Edward and Bella, she soon fell asleep.

She woke up with a start as the doorbell rang. It was 6 a.m., too early for the milkman. Who could it be, she wondered. Quickly getting out of the bed, she got into her cardigan. She tried to peer into the eyehole but it was foggy outside. As the doorbell rang again, she opened the door and couldn't believe her eyes. It was Mani standing there!

She rubbed her eyes in disbelief and gathered her gown around her tightly.

"Happy birthday, darling," Mani said tenderly and gave her a big bouquet of fresh, red roses.

"But, but ..." Ragini was lost for words.

Wordlessly, Mani took her in his arms. They stayed in that position for some time, happy just to be together.

Finally, Mani spoke.

"Please forgive me, I know what I have done is unpardonable but please forgive me. I'll try to explain but first let us celebrate your birthday. I've got gifts for you." Saying that, Mani looked at her, trying to fathom her reaction. Ragini was bemused.

"My birthday was yesterday," she said with a smile.

Mani was shocked that he had goofed up in remembering Ragini's birthday. But Ragini laughingly dragged him inside, her anger, sadness and annoyance all evaporating at the sight of the very sheepish Mani. Seeing her smile, Mani also smiled at his lapse and as they laughed together, the awkwardness between them dissolved, leaving only love behind.

Mani continued to hold and caress her and Ragini's barrage of questions were buried in the avalanche of passion that crossed all barriers. Later, as Mani made them tea, Ragini gathered her thoughts and was determined to talk firmly to Mani. As Mani handed her the cup, he apologized again to Ragini.

"I cannot even begin to explain what I went through. Sitting here now with you seems so – so natural and normal but there in Bangalore, I was under a dark cloud and my demons of past had totally possessed me. It was Varsha's thoughts and the unresolved questions as to why the marriage failed and why the whole thing ended the way it did," Mani spoke with trepidation, all along looking at Ragini's face for her reactions.

Ragini of course did not like what she was hearing and asked him, "Looks like you are still in love with her. I thought your relationship with her was emotionally over. You had shared so many of your thoughts about her with me and I had listened to you patiently, then what happened suddenly that you became so withdrawn? I can only assume that her death made you realize you still loved her and hence you didn't want to move on," Ragini said in an accusing tone.

"I know it may appear like that," Mani replied, trying to placate her, "but it wasn't simply thoughts of Varsha that were keeping me away. I was drowned in thoughts of self-doubt and kept thinking, what if I failed you as well? I don't ever want you to stop loving me and the very thought that you could go away from me was frightening."

"So you yourself went away from me," Ragini said softly, with tears glistening her eyes. Mani wiped the tears away and kissed her gently.

"I'm sorry, I was wrong. I should have shared my feelings with you. I was questioning myself so much that everything else became less significant. But sweetheart, please, now let's be together. It may be difficult for you to trust me again, but I promise that I won't ever let you down. You are the one for me and I'm free from all negative thoughts now."

Ragini stayed quiet and listened as Mani told her about the visit of Dinesh that brought him to his senses. Ragini was touched and realized she had found a loving family who had already accepted her. She had met Dinesh and Archana barely a few weeks ago, but it seemed that the bonds with his family were already strong. She told Mani how she had confided in Archana and both fell silent thinking of the past few weeks.

Mani, in a bid to lighten the mood, got out the gifts he had got for Ragini. There was a cosmetics hamper, a rust-and-gold silk suit and as Ragini looked at them excitedly, he went up to her and put a simple chain with an exquisite rose quartz pendant around her neck.

"May you always be happy, my love," he said, kissing her again.

Ragini loved the chain and pendant set and was delighted. "I'll always wear it," she promised herself and returning Mani's kisses with the same fervour, she went to the kitchen to organize breakfast.

She called Mia, excited and full of happiness. Mia was delighted with the news.

"Good he saw where his future lay," she said bluntly. Telling Ragini to enjoy the day and firm up things, she kept the phone down.

Ragini called her office and took leave. She and Mani spent a lazy day. They stayed inside the house and talked their hearts out. Ragini described how she had met Ravish and how he had tried to force himself on her. Mani was horrified and asked Ragini to immediately delete her profile from the marriage website. Ragini laughingly reminded him that he should also do the same. Both then spent some time doing that.

Ragini called up Kamini and told her how Mani was there with her. A delighted Kamini spoke to Mani and welcoming him to the family, invited him again to visit Banaras. Together they then spoke to Archana and Dinesh, who were pleasantly surprised about the turn of events. All too soon, it was time for Mani to go.

Ragini slept contentedly that night and woke up relaxed the next morning. There was a message from Mani that he had landed safely and she had a quick chat with him before getting ready for office.

In the evening, she went to Mia's house and as Mia teased her about the glow on her face, Ragini blushed. She and Mia had dinner together and Mia told her to start preparing for her wedding. "But he has not proposed!" exclaimed Ragini and Mia nodded as both friends realized the absence of a formal proposal from Mani.

"Not that it is really needed," Mia said, but the romantic in Ragini hoped that it would occur to Mani sooner than later.

Days passed as Ragini and Mani's relationship blossomed again. Mani kept reassuring her and as the winter appeared to be over, Ragini realized this spring was going to be very special.

On Valentine's Day, Ragini received a big surprise again. Mani rang her bell and he had a huge bouquet of red roses for her. As she happily hugged him, she was greeted by one of Mani's favourite numbers being played on his phone.

I love you more than I can say

I'll love you twice as much as tomorrow

Whoa whoa yeah yeah

I miss you ev'ry single day

Why my life must be filled with sorrow

Oooh oh

I love you more than I can say

And then Mani popped the question.

"Will you marry me, darling?" he whispered in her ears and Ragini was swept off her feet. She was so lost that she could not even reply.

"Ragini, Ragini," Mani called out, "I'm still waiting for my answer."

Laughing, Ragini said, "Yesssss!" and was lost in his arms as he covered her with kisses.

Mani wanted to get married quickly, and so did Ragini. Mani sought his brother and sister-in-law's help to speak to his parents and fix things up.

Mani's parents were surprised when they heard the news. In fact, they were a bit hesitant as they did not want Mani to take a hasty decision again. Mani's mother mellowed down when she saw Ragini's pretty picture. Mani's father, a retired government official who had retained his authoritative air, was quite progressive in his thinking. Wanting Mani to settle down again, he concurred with his choice and spoke to Ragini's father to plan a visit to Banaras.

Mani's family decided to visit Banaras just before Holi. Archana confided in Ragini that they were coming prepared and in all likelihood Mani and she would be exchanging rings when they met next. Ragini immediately told Kamini, who asked her to arrange a ring for Mani. Ragini picked up a simple gold band – solid and pure – and hoped their relationship would always be like that. She asked Mia to accompany her to Banaras. "Try stopping me!" answered Mia playfully and gave her a big hug.

Both girls decided to wear saris for the event and went shopping for their attire. Ragini picked up a deep-green sari with elegant embroidery and Mia settled for a royal-blue one with intricate patterns. They reached Banaras a day before Mani's family was to arrive to help Kamini with the arrangements.

As Mani's family arrived, both Kamini and Ragini had a strong sense of déjà vu. They looked at each other, both remembering Deepak Shrivastav and laughed as they welcomed Mani. Ragini was wearing the suit Mani had got for her and looked alluring. Mani looked dapper in a plain shirt and jeans. They stole glances at each other as the families settled down to talk.

Kamini liked Mani instantly. She called him aside and expressed her happiness.

"I can't tell you how happy this union makes me. Ragini has seen lot of turmoil and I really hope both of you will be happy together," she said emotionally.

Mani was full of gratitude towards her for being a pillar of support for Ragini. "I know all about her travails, Didi, and I assure you she will never face them again. In fact, I want to thank you for being there for her always. I have myself given her a lot trouble, but I will ensure that everything will always remain well between us," he promised.

Mani and Aman also hit off well. Ragini's father struck up a conversation with Mani's father and both could sense and appreciate each other's family values.

Ragini's father spoke with Mani and asked him about his future professional plans. He seemed satisfied with Mani's responses. As Ragini naughtily picked up the tray of tea cups, and stepped inside the living room to greet Mani's family, she winked at Kamini and Mia and the three smiled in contentment. It had been a tumultuous time for them but now, finally, Ragini was going to marry again!

Ragini greeted Mani's parents by touching their feet. She liked Mani's mother instantly and could almost see her own mother in her. His father looked like a disciplinarian and in him, too, Ragini thought she could see a reflection of her own father.

After the tea with hot snacks and other savouries were served, Mani's mother formally asked for Ragini's hand in marriage and there was joy on everyone's face. The talk veered around to fixing the marriage date and the family priest was summoned. Mani almost felt like asking Ragini if she had arranged with him for giving an early date but there was so much hustle and bustle around that there was no opportunity to be alone with her.

After checking the planetary positions and their horoscopes, the priest offered them three dates in April – 15, 19 and 20. It was already nearly mid-March and both Ragini and Mani simultaneously said, "15 April it is!"

"My, my, both of you have accomplished the most difficult thing in India – to convert a love marriage into an arranged one," Mia said sagaciously and Ragini couldn't agree more.

Mani and Ragini smiled at each other and realized a new future was beckoning them, a future free of the shadows of their past, where only the positive aura of love would prevail.

The families decided to have a small ring ceremony in the evening before Mani's family returned to Delhi. Mia hurriedly got Ragini ready and she looked stunning in the deep-green sari she had bought for the occasion. As Ragini stretched her hand towards Mani and they exchanged rings, Ragini felt all her dreams coming true. Ignoring the presence of all the people around them, Mani drew her a bit closer and whispered, "No more chances now."

*****

Epilogue

The Arya Samaj Mandir, Banaras, stood transformed on 15 April 2006. The vibrant hue of marigold and the soft aroma of jasmine enveloped the old temple and gave it a festive look. Ragini looked resplendent in a deep red Banarasi sari with intricate golden zardozi work while Mani was his charming best in a colour coordinated maroon and golden kurta set. "April is no longer the cruellest month," Ragini thought, her mind going over one last time about the events of the previous year. Her eyes came to rest on Mani, who smiled at her reassuringly. They had chosen a simple day-time marriage in the temple without the usual pomp-and-show involved in such events.

It was a traditional marriage ceremony that brimmed over with the magical emotion of love. There was joy among the small gathering of family and close friends who witnessed the rituals. Mia, who looked sensational in a designer outfit, could sense that Mani's cousin, Vivek, was following her around with interest and she felt inclined to reciprocate. Ragini's going away was going to create a vacuum and perhaps it was time to settle down, she thought happily. As the priest recited the marriage vows and Mani and Ragini took the seven steps of commitment, togetherness and happiness, Ragini felt tears rolling down her cheeks. Mia gently wiped her own tears away, only to see Kamini also sniffing. With a sigh, Mia looked for a tissue, which Vivek promptly offered her.

You can't force anyone to love you. All you can do is to be lovable and trust that the right one will love you back.

Law of Attraction
Dipak Chopra

ACKNOWLEDGEMENTS

I thank

My mother, Sudha, and my late father, Dr. Suresh, for the determination and grit that I inherit from them.

Manish, for being the companion that he is. Devika and Sarthak, for their resilience and all of them for providing valuable inputs as well.

Ashlesh and Sheel Ratan for being the silent supporters.

My teacher, late Mrs. S. Sen, whose words, 'Kavita, do not give up writing,' echo in my ears.

Surinder Ghai, for his faith in me and for providing a platform for Second Chance.

Sanjiv Sarin, for all the patient chiselling he did. We agreed to disagree so many times but there was a learning in each discussion.

Nidhi, for really pushing me and providing the first feedback.

Shobit, for his able and discerning guidance.

My entire family

And

All my friends

For standing by me always.

About the Author

Dr. Kavita Bhatnagar, an Indian Revenue Service officer, belongs to Ajmer. She holds a doctorate in Political Economy and has worked for over two decades in various positions in the indirect tax department. She has represented the country both at the World Customs Organization and the World Trade Organization. She has received the WCO Certificate of Merit for her contributions.

An avid observer of life, her interests in reading and writing led her to pen *Second Chance*. This is her first novel. She lives in Delhi with her family.

She can be contacted through her LinkedIn profile kavita-bhatnagar-irs.